The Joan Anderson Letter

...ance in recogniz... years. The exquisite twists ...in that they are as hopeless. Aha! ...helplessness has only tiny Action to ...countless fine creases indelibly e...ch ...aths in my mind and few that are not ...sts. It is but gentle fog thru which ...stant intimate communion. Within the ...ouch each sleep I've gained anew the ...I roll. I embrace to its exhaustion ...calm mind now mantained by my dry bri... ...you bums, all jump off the gravy-tr... ...inheritance and shove to the hilt f ...deep are the roots and deeper its n ...hy sting?

...o you; I've been cut off. I had to ...I earned but 180 bucks in last 5 wee ...ip is proving well nigh impossible. ...on of tape recorder big problem, but ...u and this fragile instrument wedded ...job here in SF to get money for trip. ...a. Poverty looms big, to be even so ...d larger luck. If I can't have car ...I shall surely shed tears for first ...e are 27 seperate items I must attend ...g south may prove neccesary with lo... ...es I struggle to straighten and prev... ...et hope all can be made well, actual ...oney. So, bah!

...eak Obispo and blank Hinkle's househo ...months, 3weeks and 10 days respecti ...le and Céline. In one sitting, poor ...rs Moby Dick from end to end, while f ...o sour--the inanely sick dialogue of ...ankering was a magnificent Modern Li ...nations. Of course, I was inclined ...ntainly picked him up offha...

The Joan Anderson Letter

THE HOLY GRAIL OF THE

BEAT GENERA- TION

NEAL CASSADY

First published in 2020
Second edition 2021
by The Black Spring Press Group
Suite 333, 19-21 Crawford Street
Marylebone, London W1H 1PJ
United Kingdom

Cover design and typeset by Edwin Smet
Proofread by Todd Swift

ISBN 978-1-913606-32-9

BLACKSPRINGPRESSGROUP.COM

Publisher's note
While every effort has been made to publish the letter exactly as
Neal Cassady wrote it to Jack Kerouac, a few decisions were taken
to benefit the general reader of this book over the scholar, especially
as some of the typing is slightly askew and the handwritten additions
are not always readily decipherable. For direct quotation, we'd still
recommend going directly to the source material (the Ur-text). We have
tried not to wilfully amend spelling mistakes. The letter, we recognize,
was written ad hoc, replete with puns, wordplay, a tease of meanings.
The scanned original is reproduced for full consultation. We greatly
thank Matt Theado and Jan Herman for help with corrections to the
letter transcript in this edition. We are open to further correction if any
slippage has occurred. Contact us at info@eyewearpublishing.com.

Introduction, Timeline
and Bibliography by A. Robert Lee.
Formerly of the University of Kent he was
Professor in the English Department,
Nihon University, Tokyo, 1997-2011.
Among his publications are *Designs of
Blackness: Mappings in the Literature
and Culture of Afro-America* (1998),
*Multicultural American Literature:
Comparative Black, Native, Latino/a and
Asian American Fictions* (2003), which
won the American Book Award in 2004,
ed. *The Beat Generation Writers* (1996),
*Gothic to Multicultural: Idioms of Imagining
in American Literary Fiction* (2009), *Modern
American Counter Writing: Beats, Outriders
Ethnics* (2010), ed. *The Routledge
Handbook of International Beat Literature*
(2018) and *The Beats: Authorships,
Legacies* (2019).

Dear Jack;

        To hell with the dirty lousy
I got my own pure little bangtail
please me yet. I wake to more hor
for now I've passed thru just repi
I have discovered new sure doom, b
the pleasure of its devulgance in
while abiding the wait of years.
terror rival Fleur de Mal in that
beyond hope,though, and my helpless
I am fettered by cobwebs, countles
There are no unexplored paths in m
the weave of my misery mists. It
and make friendly by constant inti
arising off the suffer-couch each
mm the bearings on which I roll.
gleanings with the sure calm mind
This calls for strength, you bums,
Fall to the game of your inheritan
I'm within my rights,for deep are
Lovely Life, where is thy sting?

        Dark facts I put to you; I've
for the last 10 days. I earned bu
of the car for east trip is provin
by train, transportation of tape r
death I vow to have you and this f
I must tomorrow find job here in S
to starve, as is Diana. Poverty l
entail huge effort and larger luck
tour of sad Galloway I shall surel
death in 1936. There are 27 seper
is but SF too. Booming south may r
hassles. All this mess I struggle
of plans, there is yet hope all ca
hinges on car and money. So bah!

I've had enough horseshit.
and the confines of its binding
than Céline, not a vain statement
us shudderings and nightmare twitch
is is my secret,and if I'm to find
nizable form I must tighten my grip
xquisite twists of this self-wrough
are as hopeless.   Aha! I am well
has only tiny Action to dominate.
e creases indelibly enched on the h
d and few that are not entangled in
t gentle fog thru which I navigate
communion. Within the hour from
I've gained anew the daily greasei
race to its exhaustion the night's
antained by my dry brittle soul.
jump off the gravy-train of stupidi
d shove to the hilt for salvation.
oots and deeper its norishment.

cut off.   I had to go to San Luis
bucks in last 5 weeks.   The fixing
l nigh impossible.   If I must trave
er big problem, but on the soul of
e instrument wedded within the mon
get money for trip.   Carolyn is ab
big, to be even solvent by May wil
I can't have car in NY for our wi
d tears for first time since mothe
tems I must attend before Jan.1, t
neccesary with loss of time and mo
raighten and prevent inconvenience
made well, actually it the whole t

Sketch of Neal Cassady by Carolyn Cassady

INTRODUCTION

A. Robert Lee

The Letter

> I got the idea for the spontaneous style of *On
> The Road* from seeing how good old Neal Cas-
> sady wrote his letters to me, all first person,
> fast, mad, confessional, completely serious,
> all detailed... The letter, the main letter I
> mean, was forty thousand words long, mind
> you, a whole short novel. It was the greatest
> piece of writing I ever saw, beter'n anybody
> in America, or at least enough to make Mel-
> ville, Twain, Dreiser, Wolfe, I dunno who,
> spin in their graves... Neal and I called it,
> for convenience, the Joan Anderson Letter.[1]

So, in his *Paris Review* interview of 1968
with the poet Ted Berrigan, Jack Kerouac supplies his own spoken summary for
the impact of Neal Cassady's Joan Anderson letter upon *On The Road* (1957).[2]
That the letter, dated December 17, 1950,

was in fact closer to 16,000 than 40,000 words, and likely remembered nearly two decades on through a degree of alcoholic haze, does nothing to reduce the momentousness. Even a first read-through could hardly fail to recognize the inscriptive energy celebrated by Kerouac, each story-episode, power of recall, idiosyncrasy. In fiction as in life, and even allowing for spats and fissures, Cassady holds Kerouac's gaze as though entranced. A near-mythology, understandably, has accrued.

This is not to step round the suspicion that Cassady sees himself deliberately writing not just to, but for, Kerouac. The one line of story folds into others. Digressions, quixotic, sexual, enter as of the moment. In-house asides and wordplay recur as does a deliberate spot of joke-telling. Literary names, Baudelaire, Melville, Proust, Céline, Dickens among others, he drops in as if to play to the writer in Kerouac who at one point Cassady teasingly calls his "gentle (or otherwise) reader." Spellings go askew ("philosophating" and

"Gordion Knot"). Actual history, if such it always is, gets re-steered or performed as it were. The upshot becomes a kind of epistolary theatre, virtually a found novella. But however construed there can be no doubt of its impact on Kerouac: the Holy Grail as he and Allen Ginsberg took to calling it.

Cassady's letter may evidently not be classic Lord Chesterfield, to whom he actually refers, either fine periodical sentence or (however unlikely) a guide to social decorum. But he knows well enough how to transform letter into storytelling, the authorial voice, the grasp of pace. Kerouac has not been alone in recognizing Cassady's agilities in this respect. Few, however, have shown more personal engagement of eye or ear. Here, in how the letter manages lived detail, was the model to inspire and be adapted to his own novel-writing.

"I wake to more horrors than Céline... I am fettered by cobwebs." The opening paragraph hits stride with no small panache. The effect is theatrical, an invitation to read on. Strapped for cash and car-less he almost relishes his self-guying role of *poète maudit*. How to carry his tape-recorder and, if reluctantly need be, travel cross-country by train to Kerouac in New York to act on their proposed trip? But above all, and true to his proposed calling, he finds himself summoned to tell the history announced with "Less than 5 years ago I met my true love." A call to attention, the storyteller's set-up, he thereby launches the main story thread of the Joan Anderson letter.

The particulars come thick and fast: Denver poolhall to motel, Joan as nineteen year old beauteous but already pregnant Jennifer Jones look-alike, the "yodelling screech" of Mary Lou Berle, the kindliness of the midget cabdriver. Story enfolds each. Joan's attempted suicide by the "stark cocktail" of hydrogen peroxide and ammonia and rescue from the balcony "by the narrowest of margins" and the hospital follow-ons for the poisons and then the scar of abortion, bespeaks real human drama. In a kind of perverse parallel Cassady tells the Cherry Mary/Mary Ann Freeland story, this time the sex at any time or place with the sixteen-year old more akin to comic-cut shenanigans ("I ripped into her like a maniac and she loved it"). The vignette of escaping nude through the family's small bathroom window ("nearly took off my pride and joy") belongs in *Tom Jones* or a Feydeau farce. The follow-on as lost altar boy godson to Father Harlan Schmidt, and false accusations while in police custody at the hands of Sergeant Tom Garrard of poolhall robbery and rape of Mary Lou, supply a fitting epilogue – buttressed by the Pentecostal faux-sermon. It would be hard to encounter a more eventful plot-line.

But Cassady is equally about fashioning, flow and improvisation, the writer looking over his own shoulder. The letter abounds in reflexive swerves as if to make the very telling as much the drama as the stories being told. Joan "was too good for me of course" contrasts with Joan's mirroring "I was too good for her." In remembering his callow if guilty disregard for her welfare Cassady interrupts to tell Kerouac "Goddammmybloodysoul, Jack, I just this very second remember something." He can give instructions as to the rhythm at which the letter should be read ("read slowly for a bit and have patience with my verbosity") and speak with knowing wink of his "unending trash."

Exuberance, spontaneity, is all ("I can hardly help from blurting out 20 or 30 statements right now despite resolution to condense"). Mid-way into the Cherry Mary story he announces, actually to little effect, that "I must cut this to the bone... because I haven't the money for stamps." His summary of "And so it goes, tale after tale around this Cherry Mary period" in fact does duty overall. It can be little wonder that Kerouac thought he had touched gold, a letter burnished in imaginative pulse and virtuosity. If inspiration were needed to help spur *On The Road* he had discovered it.

On The Road

Kerouac had come to *On The Road* from his first novel *The Town and the City* (1950), his would-be epic of the Massachusetts to Brooklyn blue-collar Martin family dynasty from the 1930s through into wartime America and the return home of the GIs. Drawing also on the circle that included Allen Ginsberg, William Burroughs, Herbert Huncke, and Lucien Carr, it shadows Thomas Wolfe's *Look Homeward, Angel* (1920) and John Galsworthy's *The Forsyte Saga* (1906-22). Both of these had been avid reading for Kerouac. Despite his hopes to have pitched for bold new authorship Kerouac came to recognize, and rue, that he was writing dutiful but unexciting naturalism. The one foot stolidly followed another. He may well have underestimated *The Town and the City*, but a different horizon clearly beckoned.

"My true story novels" becomes one of Kerouac's key phrasings. It well suits and with *On The Road* quite the best-known embodiment. Sal Paradise as Dean's Boswell works exactly, variously exhilarated, amazed, not a few times thrown into consternation. But always he acts as ready witness to the urge to see in Dean life seized by the throat, human appetite and energy to meet America's full continental invitation. East and West Coast, Route 66 and the Mississippi River, Chicago and New Orleans, the lure of the corn-belt Plains and "the magic border" of indigenous dark Mexico, and always the "holy-boy road, madman road, rainbow road, guppy road, any road," feed into the confessional flow of experience.[3] The Anderson letter could have no better homage, Sal ever with "my notebook" and kin to the real-life Cassady at typewriter keyboard.

Kerouac's styling of the novel lies as much at the centre of its appeal as the events it records. Dean, Sal's "young Gene Autry" who ostensibly comes into his life "to learn to write," draws him onto "a tremendous new season together." This, in one of the most celebrated passages Kerouac ever composed, is the Dean who belongs in the company of Beat's sacred ranks:

> the ones who are mad to live, mad to talk, mad to be saved, desirous of everything at the same time, the ones who never yawn or say a commonplace thing, but burn, burn, burn, like fabulous roman candles.[4]

No increment in the story lacks this edge, a style to meet the book's carpe diem ethos. The span covers Dean's beatified figuration yet HOLY GOOF through to his last ragged and thumb-injured exit, Sal's encounters with Remi Boncoeur through to the love-sojourn in the San Joaquín Valley and Sabinal with his *campesina*.

Each ensuing novel with Cassady renamed Cody Pomeray shares pitch and tempo, in turn *The Dharma Bums* (1958), *Book of Dreams* (1961), *Big Sur* (1962), *Desolation Angels* (1965), and overwhelmingly *Visions of Cody* (post. 1972), in which Kerouac transfigures Cassady "as if a superhuman spirit." In designating these and the rest of his oeuvre the Duluoz Legend, a borrowing from the family's French Canadian background, he had grounds to tell Malcolm Cowley, the legendary editor at Viking Press, that the dynamics of his writing would make him "a running Proust." The Anderson letter provides ingress, unmistakable threshold.

The Correspondent

Who, quite, was Neal Cassady? To what extent was he "the root, the soul of Beatific" as Sal Paradise calls Dean Moriarty in *On The Road*? [5] Although it deals only with his skid-row Denver childhood, Cassady's own *The First Third* (post. 1971, revised and expanded 1981) gives opening parameters.[6] The Oliver Twist upbringing he led with Neal Cassady Sr., the alcoholic father whose marriage to a woman already the mother to eight children ended in separation and whose jobbing work as an itinerant barber, meant drift and shabby one room hotels. Little wonder his son, always at the shared edge of indigence, took early to miscreant ways and the boast that between 1940 and 1944 he managed to steal as many as 500 cars (though he always maintained he only "borrowed" them for joy rides). The route into petty crime, panhandling, poolhalls, tricking "marks" for cash, Reform School, train-hops, a precipitate marriage with 16-year-old LuAnne Henderson, would also comport with the instinct for reading and story-writing begun in school and through to his prison years and beyond. Athletic, voluble, maybe even bipolar, by the time of his encounter with Kerouac and Ginsberg he had no doubt that, whatever else, his career included the writer-in-waiting.

Neal Cassady: Collected Letters, 1944-1967 (2004) fills out the compass. The way-stations have grown familiar: employment as brakeman on the Southern Pacific Railroad through the 1940s, marriage to Carolyn and the hitching and road travels with Kerouac in 1948 to include visits to William Burroughs in Texas, bigamous marriage to Diana Hansen in 1950, and the Joan Anderson letter later that year. His obsession with horseracing leads to the loss of $10,000 in bets from an investment he and Carolyn made of insurance money paid out for a broken leg sustained working on the railway. That he took out the money fraudulently was par for the course. Kerouac's move into the Cassady household in San Francisco, with its attic writing retreat and sexual imbroglio instigated by Neal, takes its course from December 1951 over several months into 1952. In the early 1950s Cassady also drafts, with copyediting assists from Carolyn, *The First Third.*

The history thereafter has equally well-known stops and starts. In October 1955 he attends the 6 Gallery reading with Kerouac and hears Ginsberg declaim "Howl." The suicide of his lover Natalie Jackson, one in his marathon of sexual liaisons, occurs in December, 1955. In February 1958 he is sentenced to two years in San Quentin for marijuana possession with a three-year parole to follow. In prison he reads obsessively, Voltaire to Dostoevsky, and the canonical authors who feature in the Harvard Classics collection. Following the divorce from Carolyn he notoriously is to be seen at the wheel of Ken Kesey's Merry Prankster Harvester School Bus with its psychedelic colours as befitted a troupe taking copious LSD and which was visited by Timothy Leary.[7] The death in Mexico in February 1968, worn, looking more than his forty-one years, and aptly by a railroad track, was literal enough. But it might with justice also be construed as both the fade, and yet the added perpetuation, of his already augmenting legend.

For Kerouac, as for Ginsberg, Cassady comes to embody the figure of life-force and resuscitation, little short of Rocky Mountain messiah. A "western kinsman of the sun," "a new kind of American saint," Kerouac calls Cassady as Dean Moriarty in *On The Road.* [8] Ginsberg, writing to Carolyn, cites Kerouac saying of the Anderson letter "Neal is a colossus risen to destroy Denver!". Each frequent memorializing photograph of the pair of them, eyes upon each other or in linked arms, gives emphasis. That does not gloss over recognition of Cassady's wilfulness, the sex-addictive narcissism with women and recurrent let-down of friends and the family he makes with Carolyn. The endeavour to arrange the brief *ménage à trois* of himself, Kerouac and Carolyn no doubt has about it an indicative turn. Yet his three offspring with Carolyn, Cathleen Joanne, Jami, and John Allen, have remembered him fondly, his genuine devotion to them. That continues to hold whether he was on the road, in prison, or generally the absentee father.

Looking back in 2011 from the English Berkshire home she had made for herself in Bracknell from 1983 onward, Carolyn Cassady was still able despite the fecklessness to recall with fondness her great love for him when at his best. He remained, she insists, wayward, but given wear and tear and the drugs never wholly dispossessed of the magnetism that first enchanted her. She also offers an important bead on his letter-writing to include the many he wrote to her:

He wrote all the time, hundreds of letters. He wrote every day. But the idea of formal writing didn't appeal to him because he hadn't gone to university. But his mind was brighter than anybody's. He read more than even Jack or Allen. In prison he did nothing but read. He had this photographic memory. As a kid he spent most of his time in the library, so he was just brilliant. What a sad ending.[9]

Beat Authorships

To invoke Neal Cassady's involvement with Jack Kerouac, be it as Dean Moriarty in *On The Road* or the co-dedicatee in Allen Ginsberg's *Howl and Other Poems* and in which "Howl" as title-poem refers to "N.C. secret hero of these poems," is to be further reminded of his enduring presence in the wider Beat gallery.[10] For the two Easterners, Canuck New Englander and Jewish New Jersey and Manhattan denizen, Cassady seemed indeed the incarnation of life risen from the frontier west, or at least from highway America and the spaces it covers. In this the car,

America's so-called greatest love-affair, acts as chariot and Cassady its fabled driver supreme.

Context for the Anderson letter and its relation to *On The Road*, requires fuller consideration of "The Beat Movement." Fact long has woven with fiction, increasingly so when seen from the lens of the Obama-Trump century. The Beat Era, with Kerouac and Ginsberg a presiding duopoly, edges ever more into period legend, replete with the laconic Burroughs as spectre, Corso as poet-wit, and Cassady its adventurer prince. The more various gallery, however, cannot be sidelined. It would, too, be remiss not to remember the role of the Little Magazine revolution in the story, mimeograph to formal page print. Beat's literary presence is unmistakable in Jones/Baraka's *Yugen* (1958-62) and *Floating Bear* (1961-71) which he edited with Diane di Prima, as it is in *Kulchur, Big Table, Moby 1, Origin, Beatitude,* and *City Lights Journal.*[11] Occasional selected extracts of the Anderson letter make appearances from

John Bryan's *Notes from Underground* in 1964 and which Neal helped run off copies, through to the online *Journal of Alta California* founded in 2017.

As the 1960s unfold, Beat morphs into Beatnik and Hippy, the emerging cultural idiom much to Kerouac's displeasure becomes one of drop-out, sex, drugs and rock and roll. In his Introduction to *Lonesome Traveller* (1960) he writes "Am actually not 'beat' but strange solitary crazy Catholic mystic." *On The Road* and "Howl" in truth tell only one part of the Beat story while happenings like San Francisco's 1967 Summer of Love, Haight-Ashbury as countercultural redoubt, squats, communes, flowers in your hair, and LSD, tell another. Evidently they connect, and Kerouac and Ginsberg remain the banner names. Both writers, nonetheless, as most of the poets and novelists usually designated Beat, were reluctant to be corralled into the one conjoined wave or ensemble.

William Burroughs, especially, was insistent on the point ("I don't associate myself with (the Beat Movement) at all, and never have, either with their objectives or their literary style").[12] Even so, and however against the grain at the time, Beat would win standing in Donald M. Allen's ground-breaking *The New American Poetry 1945-1960* (1960).[13] There the inclusion of Kerouac, Ginsberg, Corso and Orlovsky as newcomers alongside poets like Charles Olson and Robert Creeley of Black Mountain, New York School names like Frank O'Hara and Kenneth Koch, and San Francisco Renaissance leading lights like Robert Duncan and Robin Blaser, give Beat as for the first time coeval literary plausibility.

Burroughs, whose *Naked Lunch* (1959) renders the modern world in terms of matrix and dystopian dark matter, ranks as Darth Vader.[14] Gregory Corso, in early collections like *Gasoline* (1958) and *Happy Birthday of Death* (1960), enters as maverick dadaist who in "Columbia U Poesy reading – 1975" satirizes being labelled part of a generation of "filthy beatnik sex commie dope fiends."[15] Lawrence

Ferlinghetti, despite also bridling at the Beat label, is thought on the basis of his early City Lights books like *Pictures of the Gone World* (1955) and New Direction's *A Coney Island of the Mind* (1958), to be both Beat poet and Beat's publisher-in-chief.[16] In Gary Snyder, from his inaugural collection *Riprap* (1959) through to *Mountains and Rivers without End* (1996) and beyond, Beat has its allied eco-poet of the Pacific Northwest and Zen luminary.[17]

Yet other names overlap, Cassady always necessarily among them. John Clellon Holmes's novel *Go* (1952) offers an early Beat *tour d'horizon* of the Village and Lower Manhattan countercultural world with Kerouac renamed Gene Pasternak and Cassady Hart Kennedy. Herbert Huncke, as born out in his winningly named autobiography *Guilty of Everything* (1990), brings a Times Square drugs and sexual underground to the surface. The street poet Jack Micheline, veteran of both the Village and San Francisco's North Beach, writes *Rivers of Red Wine* (1957) with a Preface by Kerouac ("he has the swinging free style I like"). Ray Bremser, in *Poems to Madness & Angel* (1964), launches a Beat outlier career at the margins of theft, drugs and incarceration ("BEING ARRESTED AGAIN FOR POETRY" reads one of his Beat-inflected poems).

The circle widens yet again though still selectively to include Michael McClure as tantric poet and dramatist, Ed Sanders and Tuli Kupferberg who create the satirical rock group The Fugs, and Harold Norse as the long un-closeted poet of *In the Hub of the Fiery Force* (2003) and author of the "cut-up" novella *Beat Hotel* (1983). Allowing for friendships and much interactive support, each of these holds to their own idiom. A cannily reflexive epilogue to *On The Road*, England to America with Kerouac and Cassady reincarnated as two British would-be hipsters, is to be met in Toby Litt's post-Beat novel *Beatniks: An English Road Movie* (1997).[18]

Boy's Own and Genders

The gender implications of Beat's inaugural litany and Cassady's place as veteran chauvinist have been conspicuous from the start. *Fellahin* was Burroughs's homocentric phrase. Yet even there the complexities are many, bi- and plural sexuality, same-sex loves both short and long term. The latter most notably would persist between Ginsberg with Peter Orlovsky, a lifetime's relationship from New York's Lower East Side to Benares, Berkeley to Paris. Burroughs himself, who had a brief liaison with Ginsberg and in his last years with James Grauerholz, or Ginsberg who also briefly took Cassady as a lover, or Beat connected writers like the ex-con and storyteller Herbert Huncke and the poet Harold Norse, each bring a different Gay history and sensibility to their work.

In the case of the friendship between Cassady, who was discernibly bisexual, and Kerouac who likely sublimated his full sexuality, there can be no doubt of a male intensity of relationship, a bromance, to the point where they could seem mirror selves. Ann Charters, Kerouac's first biographer and writing in 1973, puts matters succinctly "Neal Cassady quickly became a dominant influence in Kerouac's life... almost an extension of Jack's personality, a part of his own life." [19]

Whatever this presiding chauvinism at Beat's inception, Men Only or Boy's Club and considerably personified in Neal Cassady, no longer can it be allowed interpretative dominion.[20] In this respect the eponymous Joan Anderson, for Cassady a sexual tryst to both flaunt and regret, offers a case in point. Appreciation, rightly, has grown of women's participation in Beat as significant American literary current. Few have more played their part than Diane di Prima, poet, editor, publisher, and Beat luminary, who bows in with *This Kind of Bird Flies Backwards* (1958), composes the feminist-mythic epic verse of *Loba* (1973-98), and writes the astute sexual tease and cross-overs of *Memoirs of a Beatnik* (1969).[21]

A first-hand perspective opens in women's life-writings and fiction, much again to immediate purposes Carolyn Cassady's *Heart Beat: My Life with Jack & Neal* (1976) and the expanded version in *Off the Road: My Years with Cassady, Kerouac, and Ginsberg* (1990).[22] Cassady himself, errant spouse, father, railway brakeman, jailee, and brother-partner with Kerouac, comes under a lover's eye whatever Carolyn's understandable feelings of put-upon bruise and regret. Other intimacy, with Cassady featuring alongside Kerouac, runs through Joyce Johnson's *Minor Characters: A Young Woman's Coming of Age in the Beat Orbit of Jack Kerouac* (1983) and the dynastic writing by Kerouac's daughter in Jan Kerouac's *Baby Driver: A Novel About Myself* (1981) and by his second wife Joan Haverty Kerouac in *Nobody's Wife: The Smart Aleck and the King of the Beats* (2000).[23]

The further compendium of names, their poetry and narrative, is not to be overlooked: Joan Vollmer, Joanne Kyger, Hettie Cohen/Jones, Janine Pommy

Vega, ruth weiss (the lower case her gesture to refusal of German-language capitalization), Lenore Kandel, Elise Cowen, and the songwriter and poet Patti Smith. A text like Bonnie Bremser/Brenda Frazer's *Troia: Mexican Memoirs* (1969), re-issued in London as *For Love of Ray* (1971), with its Abelard and Eloise love story might be considered a woman's south of the border counter-voyage to *On The Road*.[24] Quite beyond stereotype as muses, lovers, or based on the preferred couture of the time "women who wore black," each was also writer and artist. Anne Waldman, whose prolific output includes the acclaimed pattern-poem, "Fast Speaking Woman," and who with Ginsberg and others in 1974-5 helped co-found the Jack Kerouac School of Disembodied Poetics at the Naropa Institute in Boulder, Colorado, is to be seen as prime intergenerational figure.[25]

In giving expression to their own imaginative realm they each to one degree or another challenge the assumed usual male prerogative of Beat and give it location within the far wider span of cultural gendering. A number, even so, take on the role of homemaker, the wife or mother, much as they might have had their own arts to nourish. The instance of Carolyn Cassady is once more notably instructive given the abundance of line drawings, paintings and set-designs that reflect her training in Fine Arts and theatre-design at Bennington College and the University of Denver. Her life as an artist spans the vexed years as Cassady's spouse, his philandering and even bigamy, the raising of the three children, his jail-time, the divorce in 1963, the move to England, and the travel and gallery interests pursued through to her demise in 2013. She throws necessary light, at times riposte, on Neal Cassady as the heroic cynosure promoted by Kerouac and Ginsberg.

Ethnicities

Beat's reach, and the Cassady-Kerouac relationship within it, has been equally orbital in issues of ethnicity. If Kerouac's

On The Road invokes jazz in plenty (New Orleans with its "mad jazz" or Chicago as sax and bebop metropolis), and his *Mexico City Blues* (1959) draws its fashioning from the music's improvisational riffs (Charlie Parker he calls a "Great musician and a great/creator of forms"), then Beat also looks to its black realm of poetry.[26] Controversy has much arisen as to the words he puts into Sal's mouth about white cultural jadedness and "wishing I were a Negro... a Denver Mexican, or even a poor overworked Jap, anything but what I was so drearily, a 'white man' disillusioned." [27] Was Kerouac peddling one-dimensional stereotype?

In the case of LeRoi Jones/Amiri Baraka, his Beat phase (usually dated 1958-1962) before moving on from Greenwich Village to the black nationalist politics of Harlem and Newark and then to neo-Marxism, is centred in *Preface to a Twenty Volume Suicide Note* (1961). His *Autobiography* (1984), with necessary emphasis on African American sources says in witness "I took up with the Beats because that's what I saw taking off and flying and somewhat resembling myself."[28]

Ted Joans, performance poet, painter, trumpeter, and international traveller to Europe and the Africa of the Maghreb and Mali, and whose mantra was always jazz and surrealism, puts Beat under black inventive auspices and wit. Among the pieces gathered in *Teducation:Selected Poems* (1999) is his captivating and deliberately capitalized memorial to Kerouac ("RUNNING ACROSS THE COUNTRY LIKE A/RAZOR BLADE GONE MAD") in "The Wild Spirit of Kicks" [29] Amid the vintage Beat years Joans and Kerouac had listened to jazz in Harlem and a host of Manhattan nightspots, friendship beyond race-lines.

Bob Kaufman comes into play as New Orleans-born but eventually West Coast literary street and cafe stalwart. He assumes his place as poet of the collection *Solitudes Crowded with Loneliness* (1965), co-founder and editor of *Beatitude Magazine* begun in 1959, and creator of the surreal-anarchic Abomunist pieces.[30] Always the jazz disciple his blues poem "West Coast Sounds – 1956" offers a wry vista of Beat personnel, among them Kerouac "writing Neal" and Cassady as "Neal... On zig-zag tracks." [31]

Rediscovery and Auction

Cassady's letters, the Anderson letter foremost, has become his writer's legacy. As Carolyn attests in her Afterword to *The First Third* "He knew he was neither trained nor equipped to think of writing in terms of literary merit." [32] In this she has the support of Lawrence Ferlinghetti who in the same City Lights edition speaks of the "homespun, primitive prose" of Cassady's autobiography. [33] But the letters, busy in live detail, increasingly self-aware, invite their own regard. In this respect, too, the history of the Joan Anderson letter as artefact affords an uncanny parallel with the literal creation of *On The Road.* Once again legend is involved.

In the case of *On The Road* partial earlier drafts there may have been, but Kerouac's ferocious speed in typing up the full single-spaced version in April 1951, 125,000 words in 20 days and fuelled by coffee, knows few equals. That it required taping 120 feet of art-tracing paper into a single scroll has made the manuscript into a collector's showpiece as born out in its purchase in 2001 by Jim Irsay, owner of the Indianapolis Colts, and displayed not only at libraries and museums in the USA but France, the UK, and Japan. The *On The Road* manuscript now has its smaller but necessary companion-piece.

In May 1951, Kerouac writes to Cassady "How many times do I have to tell you the letter about Joan Anderson is an American masterpiece and so you are leaving it to ME to sweat to publish it." Seven decades on, and in the long shadow of Kerouac's promise, that has come to pass in the present edition from Black Spring Press. For the history of Cassady's own cramped and typewritten 18-page letter, actually double-sided 9 pages, resembles that of Kerouac's scroll. Available hitherto only in part, whether in the re-issue of *The First Third* or in the different journal extracts, it has become the "missing" manuscript once supposedly lost and only latterly re-found.

A compelling account of the document can be heard in a podcast of December 2014 from the Beat Museum in Broadway, San Francisco, and chaired by its founder Jerry Cimino. For an age it had been thought that Allen Ginsberg to whom Kerouac had passed the letter in turn gave it to the poet Gerd Stern in the hope he could get it published with A.A. Wyn, owner of Ace Books who had published Burroughs's *Junkie*, uncle of Carl Solomon to whom the poem "Howl" is dedicated. Stern had worked as West Coast agent for Wyn who, in the event, had no interest in publishing the letter. It was then sent by Stern to *Golden Goose*, the poetry journal edited by Richard Wirtz Emerson. Seemingly having disappeared the responsibility was attributed to Stern, that he had lost it or thrown it into the

San Francisco Bay from his houseboat moored in Sausalito.

Stern explains that such was emphatically not the case. He was right. The letter had passed from Emerson, who on retirement was about to throw out all his accumulated papers, to Jack Spinoza of the recording company Gold Coast Records which shared an office building with *Golden Goose*. In December 2011, Jean Spinoza, Jack's daughter, was clearing out her father's boxes in Oakland with the dealer Mike McQuate, and they found the letter in a manila envelope amid a host of other papers taken from the *Golden Goose* office. There, as though recovered from time and dust, was the original.

The letter Ginsberg mischievously kept saying had been lost by Stern while in truth having lain in storage for 57 years. Stern also raises the possibility that the parts of the version previously seen that had found their way into print were from a copy (typed by Kerouac?). Nor was he prepared to agree that *On The Road* wholly was inspired by the letter accentuating, rather, Kerouac's ear for jazz and the ability as both poet and prose-writer to create matching improvisatory riffs. Either way, after Jean Spinoza put the letter up for sale, there followed legal squabbles as to ownership and copyright between herself and the Kerouac and Cassady estates before auction (actually the third after the others failed to meet the reserve price) and eventual purchase for $206,250 by Emory University, Georgia, in March 2017.

The earlier Christie catalogue offered the following promotional blurb:

> Cassady left his mark on a generation of writers through the power of this one letter… its rawness and speed focused this strain of postwar American thought, drew together an immediacy of life and living with a new intellectualism, fused existentialism with the coming of the prosaic with the elegiac. And it did so by influencing the masters of the movement without the benefit of having its own critical appreciation.

Both the Heritage Auction catalogue and

the Emory University public exhibition titled "The Dream Machine: The Beat Generation and Counterculture 1945-1975," and held from September 2017 to May 2018, confirm the degree to which the Anderson letter has become a Beat literary landmark.

Perspective

Literary critique, in giving acclaim to the letter, has added helpful nuance. William Plummer, for instance, writes:

> The story proper was the least of the letter's attractions. What entranced Kerouac especially was the virile rush and spew of the style. The letter was a concoction of tones and digressions, of asides, interpolated stories, and jokes, which added up in Kerouac's mind to splendid spendthrift writing.[34]

In their study David Sandison and Graham Vickers, citing Cassady's account of the infamous window escape episode, alight on the spoken quality of the letter:

> Kerouac had found his muse in the shape
> of the man... who had now shown him a
> spontaneous style of writing – loose, rolling
> sentences studded with pin-sharp descrip-
> tions and vignettes – that perfectly suited
> his ambitions to create a written equivalent
> of "crazy jazz" rhythms and riffs.[35]

For Kerouac this drama of utterance, and
the life Cassady brings to him and shares
or on occasion maybe invents, was irre-
sistible.

Appropriately the threads that connect
the Joan Anderson letter with *On The Road*
call up the prolific other correspondence
between Cassady and Kerouac. Likewise
the lengthy circumstantial letters written
to Ginsberg ("The Ides of March and your
punk, puny Caesar Cassady, is at another of his phoney Rubicons" he writes
on March 15, 1949) or to Diana Hansen
("I haven't time to reread for mistakes or
illegibility" declares a letter on September 16, 1950), and each of those penned

to Carolyn, belong in kind with the Anderson and other letters to Kerouac.[36]
The same fervour holds, the same Neal
Cassady is to be heard in spate. As for
Kerouac he knew intuitively and virtually
from the outset that his life as novelist
had encountered its pathfinder.

NOTES

1 Jack Kerouac: The Art of Fiction, No. 41, Interviewed by Ted Berrigan, *Paris Review,* Issue 43, Summer 1968.

2 Jack Kerouac, *On The Road*, New York: Viking, 1957. Page references are to *On The Road*, London and New York; Penguin, 1972, 1991.

3 *On The Road*, 229.

4 *On The Road*, 7.

5 *On The Road*, 176.

6 Neal Cassady, *The First Third & Other Writings*, San Francisco: City Lights Books, 1972, revised 1981.

7 The classic New Journalism account of the Merry Prankster episode is to be found in Tom Wolfe, *The Electric Kool-Aid Acid Test,* New York: Farrar, Straus and Giroux, 1968.

8 *On The Road*, 19, 35.

9 Carolyn Cassady in interview with Polina Mackay, European Beat Studies Network, Website 2011.

10 Jack Kerouac, *On The Road*, New York: Viking, 1957. Allen Ginsberg, *Howl and Other Poems*, San Francisco: City Lights Books, 1956.

11 For a full context of these magazines see Alan Golding, *From Outlaw to Classic: Canons in American Poetry,* Madison: The University of Wisconsin Press, 1995.

12 William Burroughs, *The Job: Interviews with Daniel Odier* New York: Grove Press, 1970, 52.

13 Donald M. Allen, ed. *The New American Poetry*, New York: Grove Press, 1960.

14 William Burroughs, *Naked Lunch*, Paris: Olympia Press, 1959.

15 Gregory Corso, *Gasoline*, San Francisco: City Lights Books, 1958; *The Happy Birthday of Death,* New York: New Directions, 1960. "Columbia Poesy Reading – 1975" appears in *Herald of the Autochthonic Spirit,* New York: New Directions, 1981.

16 Lawrence Ferlinghetti, *Pictures of the Gone World*, San Francisco: City Lights Books, 1955; *A Coney Island of the Mind* , New York: New Directions, 1958.

17 Gary Snyder, *Riprap*, Kyoto, Japan: Origin, 1959; *Mountains and Rivers Without End*, Washington D.C.: Counterpoint, 1996.

18 Harold Norse, *Beat Hotel*, German Trans. Carl Weissner, Augsburg: MaroVerlag, 1975, San Diego; Atticus Press, 1983; Toby Litt, *Beatniks: An English Road Movie,* London: Secker & Warburg, 1997.

19 Ann Charters, *Kerouac: A Biography,* San Francisco: Straight Arrow Books, 1973, 72.

20 For relevant studies and anthologies see Brenda Knight, ed. *Women of the Beat Generation: The Writers, Artists, and Muses at the Heart of a Revolution*, Berkley: Conari Books, 1996; Richard Peabody ed. *A Different Beat: Writings by Women of the Beat Generation*, London: Serpent's Tail, 1997; Ronna C. Johnson and Nancy M. Grace, eds. *Girls Who Wore Black; Women Writing the Beat Generation*, New Brunswick, New Jersey: Rutgers University Press, 2002, Nancy M. Grace and Ronna C. Johnson, *Breaking the Rule of Cool: Interviewing and Reading Beat Women Writers* , Jackson: University of Mississippi Press, 2004; Mary Carden, *Women Writers of the Beat Era: Autobiography and Intertextuality*, Charlottesville: University of Virginia Press, 2018.

21 Diane di Prima, *This Kind of Bird Flies Backwards*, New York: Totem Press, 1958; *Loba: Part 1*, Santa Barbara: Capra Press, 1973, *Loba as Eve,* New York: Phoenix Book Shop, 1975, *Loba Part II*, Point Reyes: Eidolon Editions, 1977, *Loba: Parts I-VII*, Berkeley: Wingbow Press, 1978, *Loba, New York: Penguin,* 1998, *Memoirs of a Beatnik*, New York: Olympia Press, 1969.

22 Carolyn Cassady, *Heat Beat: My Life with Jack & Neal,* Berkeley: Creative Arts Book Company, 1976; *Off the Road: My Years with Cassady, Kerouac, and Ginsberg,* New York: William Morrow and Company 1990.

23 Joyce Johnson, *Minor Characters: A Young Woman's Coming-of-Age in the Beat Orbit of Jack Kerouac*, Boston: Houghton Mifflin, 1983; Jan Kerouac, *Baby Drive*, New York: St. Martin's Press, 1981; Joan Haverty Kerouac, *Nobody's Wife: The Smart Aleck and the King of the Beats*, Berkeley, Creative Arts Book Company. 2000.

24 Bonnie Bremser (Brenda Frazer), *Troia: Mexican Memoirs*, New York: Croton Press, 1969, *For Love of Ray*, London: London Magazine Editions, 1971.

25 Anne Waldman, *Fast Speaking Woman and Other Chants,* San Francisco: City Lights Books, 1985. 20th Anniversary Edition, *Fast Speaking Woman: Chants and Essays*, San Francisco: City Lights Books, 1995.

26 These are given fuller account in A. Robert Lee, ed. *The Beat Generation*, London: Pluto Press, 1996, and *The Beats: Authorships, Legacies*, Edinburgh: Edinburgh University Press, 2019.

27 *On The Road*, 164.

28 LeRoi Jones/Amiri Baraka, *The Autobiography of LeRoi Jones/Amiri Baraka*, New York: Freundlich Books, 1984, 156.

29 Ted Joans, "The Wild Spirit of Kicks," *Teducation: Selected Poems 1949-1999,* Minneapolis: Coffee House Press, 1999, 97.

30 Bob Kaufman, *Solitudes Crowded with Loneliness*, New York: New Directions. 1965

31 *Solitudes*, 11.

32 *The First Third*, 140.

33 Lawrence Ferlinghetti, *The First Third,* n.p.

34 William Plummer, *The Holy Goof: A Biography of Neal Cassady,* New York: Paragon house, 1981.

35 David Sandison and Graham Vickers, *Neal Cassady: the Fast Life of a Beat Hero*, Chicago, Chicago Review Press, 2006, 196-7.

36 *Neal Cassady Collected Letters, 1944-1967*, ed. Dave Moore, London and New York: Penguin Books, 2004.

The Letter

Photograph of Neal Cassady and Jack Kerouac by Carolyn Cassady

DEAR JACK,

To hell with the dirty lousy shit, I've had
enough horseshit. I got my own pure
little bangtail mind and the confines
of its binding please me yet. I wake to
more horrors than Céline, not a vain
statement for now I've passed thru just
repetitious shudderings and nightmare
twitches. I have discovered new sure
doom, but this is my secret, and if I'm
to find the pleasure of its divulgence
in recognizable form I must tighten my
grip while abiding the weight of years.
The exquisite twists of this self-wrought
terror rival Fleur de Mal in that they are
hopeless. Aha! I am well beyond help,
though, and my helplessness has only
tiny Action to dominate. I am fettered
by cobwebs, countless fine creases indelibly etched on the brain. There are
no unexplored paths in my mind and
few that are not entangled in the weave

of my misery mists. It is but gentle fog thru which I navigate and make friendly by constant intimate communion. Within the hour from arising from the suffer-couch, each sleep I've gained anew the daily grease for the bearings on which I roll. I embrace to its exhaustion the night's gleanings with the sure calm now maintained by my dry brittle soul. This calls for strength, you bums, all jump off the gravy-train of stupidity. Fall to the game of your inheritance and shove to the hilt for salvation. I'm within my rights, for deep are the roots and deeper its nourishment. Lovely life, where is thy sting?

Dark facts I put to you; I've been cut off. I had to go to San Luis O. for the last 10 days. I earned but 180 bucks in the last 5 weeks. The fixing of the car for east trip is proving well nigh impossible. If I must travel by train, transportation of tape recorder big problem, but on the soul of death I vow to have you and this fragile instrument wedded within the month. I must tomorrow find job here in SF to get money for trip. Carolyn is about to starve, as is Diana. Poverty looms big, to be even solvent by May will entail huge effort and larger luck. If I can't have car in NY for our winter tour of sad Galloway I shall surely shed tears for first time since mother's death in 1936. There are 27 separate items I must attend before Jan.1, this is but SF, too, Booming south may prove necessary with loss of time and more hassles. All this mess I struggle to straighten and prevent inconvenience of plans, there is yet hope all can be made well, actually the whole thing hinges on car and money. So, bah!

Enfolded in bleak Obispo and blank Hinkle's household for the second time in less than 2 months, 3 weeks and 10 days respectively, I had nothing to blast but Melville and Céline. In one sitting (poor ass) of 30 hours I took between my ears Moby Dick from end to end, while forcing into my belly—where it settled so sour—the inanely sick dialogue of Helen and Al. This copy of Herman's Hanker-

ing was a magnificent Modern Library giant with great pen-and-ink illustrations.
Of course, I was inclined not to enthuse
over the old boy too much and certainly
picked him up offhandily for I'd read it
all long ago. Then too, the new school
hangup (remember a certain lecture we
attended on MD?) and all the hustlebustle of his recent rediscovery made me
pretty sure I wouldn't find another mystery to delve, and I didn't. I simply had
a nice ordinary period of reading except
that as I read I replaced certain words,
admired others, and all in all went thru
the thing as one author digging another for help, yet critically. One new impression, especially when compared to
long-ago reading; he is simple, writes so
simple and is very simple to understand.
It's wonderful that he is so, would that
I was as clear, would too that I had his
strength as I have his philosophy and
death knowledge. Céline too, I knew
again, hasn't got it like good ole Tommy
boy, yet Ferdy is purty and his humor's
a zoomer. Naturally, there is nothing I

can tell you about this trio (long tom, big tom, lunging plunging gaping gulping grasping gone gurgleboy tom, but best; Tasty Tommy. Dirty Ferdy, filthy ferdy, lousy louie, looney louie, lecherous louie, lazy louie, lucky louie, blue Lou, limpin' lou, ad infinitum or ad nauseum or et al or etc or on and on and so forth about huge herman, humpback herman, hardy herman, hasty herman, hamstrung herman, healthy herman, hallalulah herman, Spermy Hermie—dammit, I saved the best name for Melville until last, and in fact got the idea for this whole parentheses from it, now what? I just forgot it completely that's all, fapdratit).

– that's a period, whazza matter. You can't see or sumpin? (flap for flappy)

Less than 5 years ago I met my true love. The winter of 1945 had already buffeted Denver for a considerable time when this momentous event occurred. Still retaining the shreds of the imposing position held some years before by unceasing philosophating, I was engaged in stretching the rags of my regal robes

over the remnants of old pupils. This I
did to exist. Those young hoodlums to
whom I'd once been master had turned
to other things, and it was a hard task
to convert their weakened concern
into crumbs of refuge. Now the juice of
preachery was withered into dry appeals
for generosity. The weather forced mornings in the library, afternoons in the
poolroom, evenings at the bar. Copious
with words and hunger I would leave
the readingroom's quietude and hurry
three short blocks to the poolhall. Here
I lolled on the hard onlooker's bench,
waiting for a mark. When an approachable one did show, and I succeeded, I
would prolong the meal he bought me.
Otherwise, and also, I subsisted on stolen candy bars and an occasional free
pop. Come evetide I attached myself to
the first available group touring the tav-
erns—preferably in a car. It so happened
that the week or so prior to meeting my
oneheart I was sleeping in the begrudged
sanctuary of a former student's automobile. On the morning of The Day I awoke

in a particularly frigid state cramped upon the backseat of the unheated car. This, and the stress of previous months of such existence, almost made me decide to take off my hairshirt for awhile. Lying there, I contemplated for a bit the possibilities of so doing. Then this image on my mind's surface led me to recall that the day held a major event. It was a semi-permanent setup I had with my younger Bloodbrother, an almost weekly change of clothes. I quickly unhinged myself and made for his home. Winter stillness froze my ears and sharp rarified air burned my throat as I pounded the pathway of the skeletonized public park bordering on the benefactor's. Entering the house in the usual fashion via a third story attic window I had to again prove my unusual skill at climbing. As a boy in eastside Denver I bettered every tree that I saw was worth conquering, save one old giant which resisted by efforts for years, until one fine night when I was well past the tree-climbing age— but, that is another tale to be told at

another time. Kneeling in the garret dust
and restraining my quickened breath as
best I could to prevent detection by the
jazzy jealous woman he called mother,
or the bull-necked liquor salesman stepfather, I rapped a soft signal over my
clothes agent's bedroom. He came up
shortly and soon I was inside the too-big
trousers and supplementary equipment
he'd brought. Once again he marveled in
undertones that I'd achieved my difficult
route made now impossible, he reasoned
by the wet snow clinging to my narrow
clutchholds. Pleased, I departed with
care to avoid excessive strain to my borrowed finery. The toll of my improvised
ladder was not too high and I found it
exacted but a few small damp spots after
dropping to the ground from the last of
the useable building ornaments.

Now, on the preceding evening I had
been occupying the rumble seat of a
friend's roadster as he eased along
downtown streets, in second gear, looking for a pickup. Driving slowly around
the corner of 15th and Tremont Sts., we

spied a likely blonde swishing across the intersection. Robert Parlez parled to the lovely and she bounced in at once. Off we flew to the outskirts and a particular field just beyond the city limits. I got the broad's phone number and then played the stranger so if Bob's hasty, and usually undenied, assault failed I wouldn't be too fouled up when I called her later. Well, he more or less made out and we all drove back to town in half-amiable spirits. Before we dropped her at a hotel in the 1300 block on Broadway she had laid down a sloppy story about losing her purse and being completely broke. Bob wouldn't part with a sous and I had none, so it did her no good to babble on. I decided to fall by her hotel room the next day if there was nothing better to do at that time.

And I did. After leaving the clotheshound I started for Broadway. Nearing the hotel I realized I was almost beside the Emily Griffith Opportunity school where a certain friend I had made while attending classes last year was about to break from a class. I thought it better to bypass Broadway for the moment and lounge in front of the school on the chance I might see him and get some coffee. I rounded the corner and saw my friend at once. He was leaning into the window of a 1940 Chevrolet sedan parked at the curb.

I was introduced to the soldier behind the wheel who was the car's lone occupant. His name was Kenneth Collins, a stocky tough looking little guy who had known my friend for years. He was on a 10-day pass and looking for women. I told him I was on my way to a girl's room and said he could come along and take over if he wanted to. He liked the idea and we drove to her place, went up the stairs and knocked on her door. At first she told me to go away and refused to open, but I talked for a few minutes and she gave in.

I walked into the room and saw a vision. A perfect beauty of such loveliness that I forgot everything else and immediately swore to forego all my ordinary pursuits until I made her. Desire intensely burned from my stunned eyes when I met her first glance from those light brown cowpools. Then I knew who she was, Jennifer Jones, only much more voluptuous with full tits and rounded ass. Amazing! A perfect real reproduction of Jennifer Jones on the edge of the bed. Oh Jack, everything went along so nicely, as I think of it I just bubble. What I mean is that the other babe, whom I'd met the night before, and Kenny hit it off great right from the start and this left me free to devote my whole mind to Jennifer. In fact so powerfully did I make myself felt that all four of us soon knew there was to be little bullshit between us and instinctively we all tried to cure our souls by a pure affair. JJones name was Joan Anderson, she came from a small midwestern town some weeks before on the first trip she'd ever made. She was approaching 20 and very innocent. The virginity of her entire nature shone thru to me as clearly as a virtue, altho I saw she was nearly 5 months in pregnancy.

Within an hour this incredibly shy creature was bashfully installed beside me in the booth of a jumping joint. While Kenny and his box danced, Joan unlimbered to my massage and as she floated on her gentle comedown I was bursting to blow. We soon left the bar and slipped into K's snug Hotel where they at once retired to bed with a bottle. I was commissioned to take K's car back to his brother's and Joan accompanied me. My excitement as I drove penetrated Joan's belly and she began to approach the peak I was on. The long return walk contained all the combination of illusions that makes young blood so prone to boil. One of those rare periods of sensation everyone has felt, the air, the girl, the hope. She put me straight on her condition; usual stuff, hi-school boy she'd known for years, first time, left home because it started to show, etc. Sad and weeping for so long, her eyes had disremembered sparkle. The talk sure knowledge vowed of our eternal union made but sparks of splintered joy come out of her twin suffered flintholes.

Back at the hotel we walked into a bounding bed on which K and his partner were going at it in a big way. They didn't pause for greeting or in any way acknowledge our presence, just kept ripping away at 60 per. I was twitching with eagerness as Joan and I snuck into the offside of the double bed. I didn't rush, didn't push, (much) didn't force and only held her in firm tender caress. With one hand gently clasping her bottom and the other supporting her back I kissed the sweet face and lips then progressed my mouth into the heavy breasts, while my enormous cock slid under the silk slip and pounded against the soft belly pressed under me. She was still so young the couple beside us bothered her, so I did not fuck then, but kept at what I was doing for an hour or so. Finally K and his left us to go eat and we were alone, yet I wisely contained myself from all-out attack for we had been tense for so long and the edge of the thrill worn off just enough so that to do it now would not please her perfectly. I pointed this out and she agreed later that night would indeed be wonderfully right.

K and girlie came back and we all went jumping on his money. Joan and I were in fine accord and her eyes were now shining full with joyous love. We planned and planned, there was no limit all we had to do was begin.

The next morning, after a night of licking the platter clean, K decided he'd had enough of his lovely and abruptly kicked her out. I could have stayed on with him for the few days before he went back to camp and I sadly needed a roof for each transient night, but Joan must stay with her friend until she was settled and, not to leave my mate, I followed the girls into the icy streets.

Neither of them knew a connection for some loot and mine had been pushed to the limit where they would have guffawed loudly at my asking for an actual cash dollar, especially for a silly waste like a hotel room. We walked for some time, then, offhand, Joan mentioned a cab driver who'd tried to father her some weeks before. She recalled his name and I got her right on the ball. Making contact by cab phone she arranged to meet him at 4 o'clock when he got off duty. We passed the time until then (3 or 4 hours) in Kenny's hotel lobby, and when Joan left to make the meet, her buddy and I stayed there to be out of the cold. Our most optimistic wishes were more than confirmed as my beauty returned in good time with money in her purse and supper in her mixer. The old boy (about 50) was really fatherly alright, happily married and with an amount of dough, he just gushed with pity at my poor innocent's plight and his wallet was touched, too. Knowing I could sneak in and out at any hour in my old haunt, (one of many such) the Denver hotel, I told the girls to rent the cheapest weekly room there. Then began the tragedy.

Purposely I have not said much about Joan's girlfriend, the one I'd met

first you understand. Altho she wouldn't
give out with it on the initial night, the
next day her high nasal twang proclaimed the name of Mary Lou Berle.
I had spent the winter of 1942 in the
Ozarks and knew her hometown of Big
Springs, Mo. and without another ear
to bend that was familiar with that section of the country, her homesick mind
really poured the blurb to me. A couple
of years before, at 16, she'd left home
and hitchhiked to Springfield Mo. and
got a job on the local radio station singing those horrible hillbilly songs every 6
A.M. This didn't last too long and she'd
tramped here and there in the Midwest
until she met Joan and together they
had Greyhound together to Denver. Let
me tell you, boy, I know there is nothing like a fine old mountain ballad, but
when Mary Lou got drunk (nightly) and
began "The Maple on the Hill" in yodeling screech, as her frosty blue eyes
wept buckets, my cringing belly would
curl into a genuine Gordion Knot. Not
that she wasn't a lovely; blonde hair

well bleached, smooth facial features, altho pancake madeup skin was much too dry, 5'2" figure, but the too-small breasts were more than compensated by the oversize ass so her weight, I judge, while just outside 123 3/4 lbs. did not yet, I suspect, approach 125 lbs., unless of course my hasty estimate is inaccurate, then naturally I allow, nay, urge, that you draw your own conclusions about her avoir du pois. Amen, and may god rest ye merry gentlemen. Speaking of Miss Berle's behind I must say here that the one quality of it, indeed, the sole property by which I remember her whole body, was an exquisite overfleshiness that is not too often found. The tempting jelly of her physical self paralleled her entire spiritual being in that the excessive soft mass made for too much matter thru which to wade, and this adequate defense defeated my most wonderfully casual attack; since I was not a perfect fool. We became buddies with our guard up.

Installed in the Denver hotel Joan and

I continued our bliss for the first few
days. We planned a highway walk soon
to Ft. Collins where I was to drive truck
and she would work at some little available thing. Able to move in my hat, I had
quickly gotten my gear together, Joan
washed her few clothes, packed them
in her one suitcase and we decided we
were ready. Nonetheless, since we still
had 3 or 4 days of free rent left, we continued in much the same routine. Joan
was quietly content to stay in the hotel
room most of the time, she sewed baby
clothes and read a bit from the books I
had. Mary Lou was quite another way,
early in the day she left and made the
bars looking for men. I followed my usual habits, poolhall; occasional chiseled
meal, drink, car ride, show, snooker
game. Going about this business I began
a depression which sharply contrasted
with the Joan idyl. This, intrinsically,
was to be expected, only perhaps not
so soon. I knew, intuitively, I was not
the one for her, not now anyhow. She
was too good for me of course, but all

that sort of thing means nothing, and besides, depends on the way one looks at it. My particular viewpoint opposed the warp in both of us, the shame was, being young and hard, I could become unmitigatingly brutal while morbidly suffering my love's pathos.

Quickly it happened, and so powerfully that after I broke the opening dike there seemed no way to plug the gap and I was helplessly embroiled and carried away by the plunging torrent from a bursted dam. Seldom have I experienced more emotion and never have I witnessed a girl's heart being broken so completely.

I had returned from the poolhall about 7 PM. Entering the girls' fifth floor room (top floors of hotels are always best) I found Joan, Mary Lou and a tough young sailor she had picked up. Mary L. was half-drunk, the navyman slightly, and Joan not at all. (as I recall J. neither smoked nor drank, being a lady she didn't cuss either.) I called my love aside and out of the blue told her I'd been thinking it over and maybe it would be better if she went to Fort Collins alone when the rent came due tomorrow. Straight off her complexion changed, pale lips quivered, then grimaced as tears sprung. From out of incredulous eyes came stricken disbelief. I decided to take a bath. I had barely gotten in the hot tub when Mary Lou stormed along the short hallway and pounded on the bathroom door, yelling to be let in at once. I opened to her and without preamble she tore into me at a furious rate. "Joan just told me you were leaving her and she's sittin' in there crying fit to die. You son-of-a-bitch. I knew you had a dirty look in your eye when you called her out in the hall. You goddamn bastard, get up out of that tub and go in there and tell her you didn't mean it, you lousy cock-sucking prick, or else I'll beat the shit out of you, and if I can't do it I'll get my boyfriend in there to help me and we'll pound your face in together, you motherfuckin' cheapskate." She went on and on, getting hot-

ter every minute and coming up with a
really fine collection of words, a string of
names for me poured from her angry red
mouth that still tingle the brain. At first
I tried to reason with her, then I got a little mad and asked her by what manner
of presumption did a stupid whore like
herself justify preaching to me, especially in such bitchy threats? This almost
did me in good; I saw at once I'd made
a mistake. She bellowed out, "right?
threat? Why you stinking bum, I see the
way you're treating that fine girl and you
expect me to just stand there? It doesn't
matter what I am, you chickenshit little
yellowbellied bastard, but, by god, I'll
show you who I am!" And with this she
pounced on me. Standing in the slippery
tub, I had difficulty holding her off right
away and she got in a couple of good
licks before I could halt her onslaught.
As she scratched my nude body while
struggling to get her hands free from
my grip, I kept worrying that she would
take it in her head to give me the knee.
She didn't, just shoved her beet face up

to mine and sputtered, "threats?", over
and over. I had her under control soon
enough, but daren't let go; at one point
she did manage to break away for a moment by biting my shoulder and then
suddenly lowering her head to deliver
a strong butt to my midriff. I "ooffed",
but caught her again before she could
get the door unlocked. Finally she tired
and I said I'd let her go if she promised
to sit down and talk sensibly. The little spitfire agreed and sank to the stool
(not the toilet, you silly ass Mr. Kerouac,
but a simple small wooden three legged
stool, 13 inches high; milkmaids made
them famous in the 18th century and
many cheap hotels place them in their
bathrooms to have the guests put all
their cloths and bath paraphernalia in
a proper heap; accommodations!) with
exhausted murder burning from her dis-
dainful eyes. Well, you can wager your
ass I talked fast. I cloud see my ittzy-bit-
tzy lovespat might begin to assume mon-
strous proportions, not only would M.L.
and her sailorboy be happy to give me a

working over, but it could even happen that I'd be kicked out in the cold Denver night. Foolish boy that I was, these wcre the simple fears in my mind as I dressed and returned to the room with Mary Lou to put out the fire. Little did I guess that the night was to gallop from this small flareup onward until at the darkest hour we would all be engulfed in hellfire and when dim dawn first declared itself, singed (I say, bud, that's singed with a d, you understand) to doom, I was to be scourged by nightmares of my clinker soul.

Joan seemed too easy to placate. I was suspicious and tho nothing but romance had passed between us before, thus giving me no previous ground upon which to base a judgement of her natural reaction to harshness, my rebuttal had hurt her too much for the present calm to be genuine. Before I began blurting a mealy-mouthed apology, before, in fact, I had hardly opened my blubber-blabbers she stopped me with, "it's alright, honey, I've forgotten everything already."

I did, however, mumble through a nice cozy job of "forgive me." The whole thing was too easy, as I said, and being leery of her quietude, I felt further explosions beneath her outward composure. I only wished, a vain punk that she would content herself with a martyr attitude so that I might be spared the bickering of an emotional young girl. Had I not avoided her pain-filled eyes perhaps I would not have been guilty of such a gross underestimation of this woman's character.

Joan urged me to go back and finish my bath and I did. While washing I realized even more fully how I'd put my foot in it and dreaded to face her when I returned to the room. But she came to face me, that is, as I was dressing after the bath she knocked on the door. Her haggard features were in strained repose as she entered and I saw that she was about to break down again. She began quietly enough, asking what I was going to do now and if I'd come to Fort Collins and see her sometime. I protested that I'd go there with her, or whatever she wanted, but it was no good, she read the lie in my eye. Slowly she wept, deeply she wept, long lashes could not contain the eyes' lament. Even were I nice enough to stay with her, she told me, she knew why I didn't love her. I was too good for her and she wasn't good enough for me. (all right now, you sloppy critic Jack, stop reading. That last sentence, to put you in the know and set the matter straight so you can intelligently point your finger at it and giggle like a silly French fool—you better have orgasms reading this, or bawl like a baby—is the crux of the whole thing. Yessir, she thought I was too good for her and believed it so strongly that all the subsequent happenings follow from this single idea. Remembrance of my Joan's thinking she wasn't good enough for me—so stupidly juvenile, hopelessly romantic, intellectually blind and such a preposterous untruth that I'm convinced it will save her soul—is the reason I write you this.)

I was stunned, even shocked! I knew

she must be joshing, but I saw no joke
in her eye. "What?" I said, "you're kidding, you don't know what you're saying, I'm a full bastard not a half-breed.
Where are your eyes? your mind? can't
you guess what a filthy rat I am? Don't
be silly, look at yourself, you're wonderful, perfect and so good it amounts
to dumbness. Stop this hogwash,
sheer nonsense, why, a hundred of you
couldn't hold a candle to my evil."

You get the idea, Jackieboy, I put it on
thick because I was really surprised. It
all did no good, she clung with stubborn
perversity to the "no good" theme in one
form or the other. Becoming more deadly
serious, as more than an hour steamed
by in that overheated bath, her intensity
at last gave me the clue for which I had
been groping since she'd first uttered
that emotionbacked statement. I'd obviously disregarded all preceding hints by
her embarrassed and retiring manner
as simply the ordinary guilt suffered by
an introverted girl experiencing her first
wrong. One could clearly see the effects

of her pregnancy had made her a frightened lonely little girl who fairly melted with shame. Noindeedy, there was no doubt as to the true nature of her flaw, a schoolboy would even sense it, and although I'd known she felt guilty above all else, I hadn't much bothered about it. After all, one sees young ladies (not used advisedly; the word ladies I mean, you drunken T headed ignoramus.) like that daily and it is the accepted—demanded, by golly—normal way for them to feel and act when in Joan's position. (everyone applaud Dr. Cassady.) It was just that I hadn't guessed the enormity of her guilt-feeling. The immensity of it struck home with all its glory. Suddenly, as I sat there, (me on the stool and her perched on the toilet cover; got that this time?) listening to this beautiful young female tear her sweet heart to ribbons because her gentle mind could not cope with the overwhelming fear that disgrace had brought to her, I knew she was lost. All had come about when a sallow kid's cock dribbled 2 seconds of sperm, which

she hadn't enjoyed, into her spicy nest—
the fragrance of which I was smelling at
that moment. As she droned on, almost
oblivious to me now, I stared into her
soul. My Joan would never know peace
again, the germ of the present insur-
mountable preoccupation with self-debasement planted in her by unwitting
parents had blossomed into the bloom
that splits the mind. I bemoaned the loss
of this child.

Abruptly, Joan said, "I love you, Neal,
goodbye" and dashed out the bathrm. I
stayed in my stooled position, cramped
with a vision of unnecessary waste. Absorbed in vacantheaded digestion of the
sad sickness in her mind, I failed, at
first, to hear the scream. Then I heard
two anguished wails, "Neal, Neal." I
jumped up and opened the door with
real terror encased in my bowels. It was
Mary Lou, tears gushing down her cherry chipmunk cheeks smeared her horri-
bly thick face powder. I saw the ghastly
stain of death shoot out from stricken
sockets, puffed lids enclosed beady eyes

of accusation. "What have you done to her? Why did you do it? What did you say, what did you say?" She raved on, standing there in the hall, her unbelievably blownup face now bent into the quivering palms of dirt-black hands. She was all in a lump and slobbering in hysterical panic. I shook her, "what happened, what happened?" I could hardly believe this silly cunt would become so scared just because, as I suspected, Joan had gathered her things and left. For a minute or two I was able to get no coherency from her, she threw herself on the filthy floor carpet all in pieces. As I dropped her and started for the room she rose up to screech, "She's dead, she's dead, and you killed her," then fell back to her sobbing.

I didn't hurry, there seemed no need to. Walking the short corridor my thought was, "why aren't there any people? With all this noise there should be heads out every door making a hellofa racket themselves just finding out what the fuss is about." So Joan has killed herself; I opened the door calmly. There was the sailor, leaning out the window, breathing hard. No words were spoken, I started toward him and then saw he had Joan's feet in his hands. I hurried to help and together we pulled her back into the room, her dress was over her head and I looked at her damp crotch, so dark and tempting, as I tugged on her delicious legs. The sailor stared, too, but was somewhat embarrassed I do believe. We laid her on the bed and smoothed her garments. Green foam was on her lips, her eyes were closed, she was lying motionless.

Now, as I told you earlier, Mr. JLK, the blonde Mary Lou was that way only by regular dousing with bleach. The sailor (no name) said that my raven-haired Joan, really most deeply black, had come into the room and evidenced an interest in MLB's bleach bottles, reading the labels, asking if they were indeed poisonous, etc. There were two bottles, one, hydrogen peroxide, and the other, spirits of Ammonia. They both, naturally, were ones of danger, and altho she gulped of both bottles, she drank mostly of the Ammonia. Gasping from the effects of her stark cocktail, and already vomiting out her stomach's contents, she pretended to let the sailor and Mary Lou help her. As soon as Joan was seated Mary Lou had rushed out to announce her death. Taking advantage of this momentary diverting of the sailor's attention, Joan had jumped up and scrambled for the window determined to throw herself out. Needless to say the sailor seized her number sevens, lucky size, as they were disappearing from view and managed to hold on until I arrived. By the narrowest of margins he had saved her, by the merest of coincidences he was in the room at all, and now by the slightest of signs I watched her return to life. She stirred, moaned, and was soon puking again, all over the bed, herself and the floor. We were easing her wretching as best we could when the door opened and in walked swollen Mary and two big men.

They were the night manager and his assistant, whom M.Lou had summoned when she had finished mopping the hall floor with herself. To my surprise neither of them were gruff or threatening at all, instead they tried to soothe everything over as if it was their fault Joan had attempted suicide. The room was a mess, everything topsy-turvy, and these big lummoxes must not have known there were hotel maids every morning, for they began hustling about, picking up things and cleaning in a frenzy. The sailor and I pitched in to help them, as Mary Lou patted Joan's sunken countenance. Bustling around straightening rumpled rugs, righting overturned chairs, emptying ashtrays and the like, I kept thinking how strange this was. Surely I could be doing something more productive than wasting time stumbling about a room that would be taken care of in a few hours anyhow by women hired for just such a purpose. I began to work up a little fantasy that I shouldn't be doing this; what would the union say, putting

* Publisher's note: we apologise for any triggering this word may cause, we include it only for historical accuracy.

a poor n*****r* out of a job. I must emphasize how really friendly these hotel men were; even if we didn't have any money we could stay on after tomorrow if Joan was too sick to move, they would call a doctor if we liked, told us not to worry about the disturbance we'd made, etc. They didn't quiz the sailor and myself being in the girls' room at midnight, didn't mention suicide and acted as tho Joan had just fallen ill from something she ate, and in fact, soon left us to our own devices as they bowed and smiled out the door.

Sometime before the December events I'm reciting—in the late spring of 1944, May and June to be exact—I drove a truck delivering laundry supplies. My employers, the Carmen distributing Co., had large barrels of Ammonia. One of these I spilled while handling one day. I'm sure you've smelled liquid spirits of A., but perhaps not had your nostrils exposed to a large amount of it all at once. The considerable quantity of ammonia that gurgled out of the barrel, even tho

I wiped up most of it, made me sick as hell as I worked over the puddle all day. Being so conditioned, when I entered Joan's follyroom I found it honest torture to endure its potent aroma. Don't think I'm one to give out with a lot of bullshit about a smell, although I wish, of course, that I could blow about one for 20 pages like Proust did. But I got to tell you that second only to the "no good" speech of Joan's this ammonia kick is the closest to my remembrance. From the first whiff my head ached, my ears pounded, my eyes burned, my heart banged against a heaving chest. And it grew worse the longer I lingered in that accursed room.

Meantime, Joan was very sick; the weak angel muttered constantly and was not entirely conscious. We debated getting her to a hospital, but didn't, we argued over giving her an antidote, but didn't; we discussed how badly ammonia poisoning might affect one who had survived more than an hour and were optimistic that she had been regurgitating

steadily. Never having heard of anyone
dying from consuming "more than half
a qt. bottle" (as Mary claimed) of spirits
of A., I talked us all into a more hopeful
idea that she would just be sickashell for
a while; placing much emphasis on the
fine puke job Joan was doing. So happy
did they become, except, of course, my
stupored Joan, that the quiet sailor said
he may as well go out and get another
bottle of whiskey. All my body hated to
leave the heated building at 2 AM, but I
knew I'd combated that damn deathagent, Spirit of Ammonia, long enough
(incidentally, the smell didn't seem to
bother the other two much) and besides,
this was my best chance of breaking
away from the hasslebeast Mary Lou. I
reasoned Joan wouldn't be good for anything the rest of the night and if I felt it
was necessary I could always come back
later to help her get treatment at Denver General Hosp. So I told the sailor I'd
accompany him on his errand, since I
needed some air. He said OK, Mary Lou
didn't seem to mind, and so I left my

limp lover laid low.

Once outside, I let the sailor know I'd see him later, if he was still in the room that night, and took off up the morning streets. In the back of my mind I had been bickering with the idea of busting in on Kenny Collins' sister. I couldn't bring myself to wake her at this hour until after I'd tramped the cold for quite a while. The poolhall and bars were closed, but I easily might have found some warm spot to lounge in, apt. houses, etc., if it hadn't been that I was holding out for a bed to flop on; especially with the outside hope of a girl in it. The trouble was I only knew her casually, I met her when, a few days before, Kenneth stopped by to feed both of us at the restaurant where she was a waitress. I knew her address, it was the same hotel Ken had stayed in; I even knew her room, number 313. There was no difficulty getting in the hotel and there was only a night clerk. I found her door and knocked carefully, she opened without even asking who was there. Seeing she recognized me, (I had been afraid she wouldn't, since she wore very thick-lensed glasses) I started an exciting tale of drink and suicide to get her interested. Ending with big complaints about my horrible ammonia illness, having no money, etc., I asked to sleep on her floor. She was amiable enough, but to allay the fisheye I thought I glimpsed under her hairless brows, I gave quick promises to try no tricks in the dark. This must have pleased her and she said sure, only come on to the bed, "because I have no blankets for the floor and I can take care of myself if you pull anything funny". Ordinarily I am not one to diddle away much time under these circumstances and I lay it to them right away, and this one was so easy too, but better than miscue, I protected my interests by going to sleep. We got up about noon and I walked her to the café, and my interest paid off, she bought breakfast. We jawed a bit, then I sauntered to the poolhall.

When I checked in some of the boys asked what was new, I said nothing and held my peace. I'd buttoned my lip because I wanted to mull over the whole last 24 hours. This sort of thing was habit, I often spent entire PM's sitting there, and while watching the finesse of the billiard players, the cash of the pool players bashing into their game and the cautious click of the red balls the snooker players favored, mused. All the games going at once nagged for my attention so that my distracted brain had developed the practice of escaping into the oblivion of ponder. Faroff wonderings at life to contrast with nearby obvious enchantment at display of skill. Vague fancies gave complicated angle-shots off my skull, as plain spheres get questick banked off the green-clothed hard rubber. I decided to return to the Denver hotel.

On the way up to my room the night manager stopped me to say my friends had left that noon. They were gone. I questioned him; Joan had been hauled away in an ambulance about 10 AM, he didn't know who called it or from what hospital it was, and Mary Lou had departed shortly after. The sailor wasn't mentioned. I thanked him and went back to the poolhall, it was now about 7 PM and I had to start conning a place to sleep. There were no prospects, so I left to get to KCollins sister by 10, the time she got off work. I spent that, and several succeeding nights with her and didn't goofoff this time, but went right to it. Altho she was a pure Okie her charms were very real and we got along OK. There was no fumbling, she fed me when I walked her to work each 2PM and again when I met her at 10; between these hours I haunted the poolhall.

One freezing afternoon, about a week after my new routine had begun, a taxicab doubleparked and its short driver pushed into the place. I saw this uniformed midget talk with the proprietor then walk straight for me. He asked if I was Cassady and said he had a message for me, "Joan Anderson is in room 9 at St. Luke's hospital and wants you to visit her." He turned and left before I

could thank him. Because I'd been lucky
enough to get inside the pants of a few
St. Luke nurses (this before the Gullions, too) I happened to know that hospital's visiting hours; so saved a nickel,
or a walk. I knew it was too late to go
that day and decided to go the next, but
hungup in the poolhall the next day, I
didn't go. Nor did I make it the following
afternoon; I kept hoping for a buddie
with a car to be available about 2:30
when I showed up at the PH, and there
was never one there before visiting hours
were over—about 3:30 or 4, I forget now.
The walk was only about a half mile, but
I keep thinking maybe a car would turn
up in a day or two so I could avoid the
cold. Well, a car never came and I was
reduced to saying to myself, "I'll go tomorrow anyhow". But I never did until—

Goddammybloodysoul, Jack, I just
this very second remember something.
Every incident in this pricky tearjerk-
er (for he who is dammed because he's
such an awful bastard) is exactly true
as I'm writing it; except one thing: What

I now recall too late to rewrite is that when I went back to the Denver hotel that next afternoon the three of them were still in the room all right, but a few minutes after I got there Joan was taken to St. Lukes in an ambulance and the man who'd arranged and paid the bill for everything was that fatherly cabdriver, the midget I speak of above. He drove M.Lou and myself to the hospital in his taxi, following the ambulance. We waited an hour or so while Joan was being admitted – I never saw her, save for those few minutes in the hospital room – then, we all left and he dropped us downtown. The point is I knew where she was all the time I was going thru the above poolhall paragraph. Now go on with this nonsense, if you've got the strength to, you must; after all you're the poor sucker who asked for it. (here comes the part where Joan's cabby comes to the poolhall to get me, the message was, "get your ass up there and see that sick girl, she's crying for you and if you don't get off your lazy butt and go yourself I'll be

in here in a day or two and drag you
there myself".) – So I went to see her.
TO MAKE THIS SOMEWHAT CLEARER:
only one message—the latter—and PH,
23 lines above, means poolhall. Please
figure it out if you can, buddy, I'm going
on.

To have seen a spectre isn't everything, one does it semi-annually, and
there are deathmasks piled, one atop
the other, clear to heaven. Commoner
still are the wan visages of those returning from the shadow of the valley. This
means little to those who have not lifted
the veil. The ward nurse cautioned me
not to excite her (how can one prevent
that?) and I was allowed only a few minutes. The headnurse also stopped me
to say I was permitted to see her just
because she always called my name and
I must cheer her. She had had a very
near brush and was not rallying properly, actually was in marked decline, and
still much in danger. Quite impressed
to my duties, I entered and gazed down
on her slender form resting so quiet-

ly on the high white bed. Her pale face
was whiter; like chalk. It was extremely apparent how utterly weak she was,
there seemed absolutely no blood left
in her body. I stared and stared, she
didn't breathe, didn't move; I would never have recognized her, she was a wax-
en mummy. White is the absence of all
color, she was white; all white, unless
beneath the covers, whose top caressed
her breasts, was hidden a speck of pink.
The thin ivory arms tapered inward until
they reached the slight outward bulge of
narrow palms, and hands in turn bent
inward with a more sharp taper only to
quickly end in long fingers curled to a
point. These things, and her head, with
its completely matted hair so black and
contrasting with all the whiteness, were
the only part of her visible. Quite normal, I know, but I just couldn't get over
how awfully dead she looked. I had so
arranged my head above hers that when
her eyes opened after about 10 minutes,
they were in direct line with mine; they
showed no surprise, nor changed their

position in the slightest. The faintest of
smiles, the merest of voices, "hello". I
placed my hand on her arm, it was all
I could to restrain myself from jumping up on the bed to hold her. I saw she
was too weak to talk and told her not to,
I, however, rambled on at a great rate.
There was no doubt she was overjoyed
to see me, her eyes said so. It was as
though the gesture of self-destruction,
in her mind, equalized all the guilt. The
courage of committing the act seemed
to have justified her to herself. This action of her conviction, no matter how
neurotic, had called for all her strength
and now she was released. Free from
the urge, since the will-for-death needs
strong concentrate of pressure to fulfill
itself, and once accomplished via attempt, is defeated until another period of
buildup is gone thru; unless, of course,
one succeeds in reaching death the first
shot, or is really mad. Gazing down on
her, with a grin of artificial buoyancy, I
sensed this and felt an instant flood of
envy. She had escaped, at least for some

time, and I knew I had yet to make my move. Being a coward I had postponed too long and I realized I was further away from commitance than ever. Would hesitancy never end? She shifted her cramped hand, I looked down and for the first time noticed the tight sheet covered a flat belly. It was empty, sunken; she had lost her baby. For a moment I wondered if she knew it, then, thought she must know – even now she was almost touching her stomach, and she'd been in the hospital 10 days – surely a stupid idea. I resolved to think better. (I've always prolonged this stupid paragraph too long for no good reason and am displeased as hell in the way the writings come out, so—) The nurse glided up and said I'd better go; promising to return the next visiting day, I leaned over and kissed Joan's clear forehead and left. (I repeat, dammit all, I didn't say a single thing I wanted to; bunk! baaa, grrrrr, horseshit.)

Off to the poolhall, back to the old grind; I seemed to have a mania. From the way I loafed there all day one would scarcely believe I'd never been in a pool-hall 2 short years before; why, less than six months ago I still couldn't bear to play more than one game at a time. Well, what is one to say about things he has done? I never again went back to the hospital to bless Joan, oh, that's what I felt like; blessing her. Each day I lac-erated myself thinking about her, but I didn't go back. "Sometimes I sits and thinks, other times I sits and drinks, but mostly I just sits". I must have been in a pretty bad way.

Anyhow, two more weeks went by in this fashion, my inability to stir from my poolhall prison became a joke, even to me. It was the night before Christ-mas, about 5 PM, when a handsome woman near 40 came inside the gaol's (so it might be misspelled, so its old English and this is modern Denver, so it's straight out of Wilde's "Ballad of Reading, Reding, Readding, Redding, goal), or right from Dickens (Charlie my boy, chipper Charlie, cheerie Charles,

Christian Charley, chuckles Chuck,
Christmasie Dickensie, etc, etc, etc.) or
a hundred others who used the word,
so it's pronounced "jail", so why not put
jail?, what a question, what a question,
what a question, you illerate immigrant,
you blarsted bum-rum bum, that is,
Bayrumbum—you marvelously married
man, any bloody fool can see jail doesn't
start with a "g" and goal does and besides showing off my learning is abso-
lutelypositivileyunquestionalbly necessary for the next word that follows it in
the gripping thriller, then too, I gotta
save "jail" for use in its proper place on
the next page, and I'll have to watchout
overdoing it, I've already put down sir,
prison and goal, so leave it in; goal, that
is.) gates and asked for me. I went up
front to meet her, as I came closer I saw
she was better than handsome, a real
goodlooker despite her age. She introduced herself, said she was a friend of
Joan (now see, that goddam goal, which
I first wrote as goal—you can easily spy
the erasure—has gotten my flappy (bot-

tom of page 1) typing all floppy) Joan-JoanJoanJoan Anderson, and invited me to dinner. My heart bounced with guilty joy, I accepted and we walked the 5 blocks to this fine though forty ladies' apt. at 162 Lincoln St. The fatherly taxi-driver opened the door, my hostess said (there I go again) said it was her husband and that Joan (careful, easy does it) said it was her husband and that Joan (careful, easy does it) would be out in a minute. Preparations for a huge dinner was in the making, I sat on the sofa and waited. The bathroom—ugly word—door swung out and before my eyes was once again the gorgeous "second" of Jennifer Jones. Fresh from the shower, mirror-primped, stepped my heroine resplendent in her new friend's housecoat. Just when you think you've learned your lesson and swear to watch your step, a single moment offguard will pop up and hope springs high as ever. One startled look and I know I was right back where I started; I felt again that choking surge flooding me as when first I'd seen her. I started talking to myself, determined to whip the poolhall rut and drag my stinking ass out the hole.

Over the prosperous supper on which we would soon pounce hung an air of excitement. Joan and I were leaping with lovelooks across the roastbeef, while cabby and wife beamed on us. As we planned, yessir, all four of us and right out loud too. I was kinda embarrassed at first when the host began without preamble, "Alright, you kids have wasted enough time, I see you love each other and you're going to settle down right now. In the morning Joan is starting at St. Luke's as a student nurse, she's told me that's what she would like to do. As for you, Neal, if you're serious, I'll get up a little early tomorrow and before I go to work we'll see if my boss will give you a job. If you can't get away with telling them you're 21—the law says you gotta be 21, you're not that old yet are you?, (I said no) so that you can drive taxi, you can probably get a job servicing the cabs. That OK with you?" I said certainly it was and thanked him; and everybody laughed and was happy.

It was further decided that Joan and I would stay with them until we got our first paycheck; we would sleep on the couch that opened out into a bed. Gorged with the big meal, I retired to the bathroom as the women did the dishes and the old man read the paper. (by golly, Jack, it seems everything I write about happens in a bathroom, don't think I'm hungup that way, it's just the incidents exactly as they occurred, and here is another one, because...) A knock on the toilet door and I rose to let in my resurrected beauty. She was as coy as ever, but removed were fear and embarrassment. We did a bit of smooching, then seated on the edge of the tub she asked if I wanted to see her scar. I kneeled before to observe better as she parted the bathrobe to reveal an ugly red wound, livid against her buttermilk belly, stretching from the navel to clitoris. She was worried I wouldn't think her as beautiful, or love her as much, now that her body had been marred by the surgeon's knife performing a Caesarian. There might have been a partial hysterectomy too and she fretted that the production of more babies—"when we get the money"—would prove difficult. I reassured her on all counts, swore my love (and meant it) and finally we returned to the livingroom.

Oh, unhappy mind; trickster! O fatal practicality! I was wearing really filthy clothes, but had a change promised by a friend who lived at 12th and Ogden Sts. So as not to hangup my dwarf savior when we went to see his buddyboss next AM, my foolish head thought to make a speedrun and get the necessary clean impediments now. Acting on this obvious need—if I was to impress my hoped-for employer into hiring me—I promised to hurry back, and left. Where is wisdom? Joan offered to walk with me, and I turned down the suggestion, reasoning it was very cold and I could make better time alone, besides, she was still pretty weak, and if she was to work tomorrow the strain of the fairly long walk might prove too much—no sense jeopardizing her health. Would that I'd made her walk with me, would that she'd collapsed rather than let me go alone, would anything instead of what happened! Not only did the new promise for happiness go down the drain, and I lose Joan forever, but her peace was to evaporate once and for all, and she herself was to sink into the iniquity reserved for a certain type of beaten women.

I rushed my trip to the clothes-depot, made good connections and was quickly on my way back to the warm apt. and my Joan. As you well know, Jack, the route from 12th and Ogden to 16th and Lincoln Sts. lies for the most part, if one so desires, along E.Colfaxe Ave. Horrible mistake, stupid moment; I chose that path just to dig people on the crowded thouroughfare as I hustled by them. At midblock between Penna. and Pearl Sts. is a tavern whose plateglass front ill-conceals the patrons of its booths. I was almost past this bar when I glanced

up to see my younger BloodBrother inside drinking beer alone. I made good
time and the hard habit of lushing that
I was so addicted to pushed me thru the
door to bum a quickie off him. Surprise,
surprise, he was loaded with loot and,
more surprising, gushed all over me.
He ordered as fast as I could drink, and
I didn't let the waitress stop, finishing
the glass in a gulp; one draught for the
first few, then two for the next several
and so on until I was sipping normally
by the time an hour had fled. First off
he wanted a phone number—the reason
for his generosity, I suspect—and I was
the only one who could give it to him.
He claimed to have been sitting there
brooding over the very girl on the other
end of this phone number, and I believed
him; had to take it true, because for the
last five months it had become increasingly clear that he was hotashell for this
chick—who was my girl. I gave him the
number and he dashed from one booth
to the other. (got that, old man? beerbooth to phone booth) I had cautioned

him not to mention my name, nor tell
her I was there, and he said he wouldn't.
But he did, although he denied it later. the reason for his disloyalty, despite
it cost me Joan, was justifiable since,
as one will when about to be denied a
date of importance while drinking, he
had used my whereabouts as a lastditch lure to tempt her out. He came
back to the booth from the booth (see
here, phone booth to barbooth, don't
you know—barbooth is a terrific dicegame for highstaked illegal gambling
in N.Denver, too, so there.) Crestfallen,
she had said should couldn't leave the
house just now, but to call her back in
a half-hour or so; this didn't cheer him
as it would have me, he's richer and
less easily satisfied. He called her again,
about 45 minutes after I had first been
pulled into the dive by my powerful
thirst, and she said for him to wait at
the joint and she'd be down within an
hour. This length of time didn't seem unreasonable, she lived quiteaways further
out in eastDenver. I thought everything

was going perfectly. Bill got the girl, I got my drinks and still had a short period of grace in which to slop up more before she showed (I certainly didn't intend to be there when she arrived) and I'd only be a little late returning to Joan where I'd plead hassle in getting the clothes. Oh sad shock, oh unpleasant time; had I just not guzzled that first beer and all, the following would not be written and I could end this story with, "And they lived happily ever after."

Whoa, old buddy, read slowly for a bit and have patience with my verbosity. (if you haven't been slowed to a stop already by my stilted style, and too, I mean more patience beyond that which you've needed for my unfunny parentheses) There are two things I've got to say here, one is a sidepoint and it'll come second, the first is essential to the understanding of the unending trash; so, I gotta bore you with one of my Hollywood flashbacks—duller, in fact. I'll leave out the most of it and be as brief as possible to make it tight, although, by the nature of it, this'll be hard—especially since I'm tired. Number 1: On June 2, 1945, I was released from Colorado State Reformatory after doing 11 months and 10 days (know the song?) of hard labour. Soon after returning to Denver I had the rare luck to meet a 16-year-old East hi beauty who had well-to-do parents; a mother and pretty sister to be exact. Cherry Mary (Mary Ann Freeland) was her name because she lived on Cherry St. and was a cherry when I met her. That condition didn't last long, I ripped into her like a maniac and she loved it. A tremendous affair, countless countless things to be said about it—I can hardly help from blurting out 20 or 30 statements right now despite resolution to condense. I'm firm (ha) and won't tell the story of our 5 months of intercourse—with its many incidents that are perculating this moment in my brain; about carnival-night we met (Elitch's), the hundreds of mountain trips in her new Mercury, rented trucks with mattress in back, at her cabin, cabins I broke into, day I got her to bang Hal Chase, time I gave her clap after momentous meeting between her and mother of my second child (only boy before Diana's) time I knocked her up; and knocked it, mad nights and early AM's at Goodyear factory I worked alone in from 4 PM to anytime I wanted to go home, doing it on golfcourses, roofs, parks, cemeteries (dead people's home) snowbanks, schools and schoolyards, hotel bathrooms, her mother's vacant houses (she was a realtor), doing it everywhere we could think of any-old-place we happened to be, in fact, we did it in ones that I can't possibly remember, often we'd trek clear from one side of town to another just to find a spot to drop to it, on ordinary occasions, however, I'd just pull it out and shove—to her bottom if we were secluded, to her mouth if not, the greatest most humorous incident of the lot; to please her mother she'd often babysit for some of their socially prominent and wealthy friends several times a week, I'd drive out to that particular evening's assign-

ment, after she called to give the address
and say the coast was clear, (funny English joke; man and wife in livingroom,
phone rings, man answers and says he
wouldn't know, better call the coast-
guard, and hangs up. Wife says, "who
was it dear" and man says, "I don't
know, some damn fool who wanted to
know if the coast was clear". Har-har-
har) and we quickly tear-off several
goodies, then I go back to work; in Goodyear truck, don't you know. We'd done
this numerous times when the "most
humorous" evening came up. It was a
Sunday night, so no work, I waited outside her 16th and High St. apt. till parents left and then went in and we fell to
it. I had all my clothes off, left in livingroom, as she was washing my cock in
bathroom (let this be a lesson to you,
never become separated from your
clothes, at least keep your trousers
handy, when doing this sort of thing in
a strange house—oops, my goodness,
Jack, I forgot for a second that you were
out of circulation and certainly not in

any need of "Lord Chesterfield's" coun-
seling—don't show this to your wife, or
tell her I offer this advice to pass on to
your son, or, if that's too harsh, to your
dilettante friends. Whew!, got out of that)
there's a rattling of the apt.'s door and
into the front room walks the mother of
one of the parents of the baby Cherry
Mary is watching, so fast did this old bat
come in that we barely had time to shut
the bathroom door before she saw us.
Here I was, nude, no clothes, and all
exits blocked. I couldn't stay there, for
what if the old gal wanted to pee, and
most old women's bladders and kidneys
are not the best in the world. There was
no place in the bathroom to hide, nor
could I sneak out due to the layout of
the apt. Worse, Mary suddenly remembered that fact that this intruder was expected to stay the night. We consulted in
whispers, laughing and giggling despite
all, and it was decided that Mary would
leave the bathroom and keep the old
lady busy while suggesting a walk or a
coffee down the street and still try to col-

lect my clothes and get them to me; no mean feat. My task was to, as quietly as a mouse, remove all the years-long collection of rich people's bath knickknacks that blocked the room's only window, then, impossible tho it looked, I must climb up the tub to it and with a fingernail file pry loose the outside screen. Now, this window, Jack, it had four panes of glass 6" long and 4" wide, which formed a rectangle of about 12 or 13" high and 8 or 9" across, difficult to squeeze thru at best, but being modern as hell, the way it was hooked to its frame was by a single metal bar in direct center!, which means when opened, split the panes of glass down the middle and made two windows. I could hardly reach outside to work on the screen—since the window opened outward—but I pushed and making a hellova noise, split the screen enough to open the window. Now the impossible compressing of my frame for the squeeze. I thought if I could get my head thru I could make it; I just was able to, by bending the tough metal bar the slightest cunthair (in those days I cleaned and jerked 220 lbs.) and of course, I almost tore off my pride-and-joy as I wiggled out into the cold November air. I was damn glad I was only on the second floor, if I'd been higher I would have been hungup in space for sure. So I dropped into the bushes bordering the walk along the side of the building, and hid there shivering and gloating with glee. There was a film of snow on the ground, but this didn't bother anything but my feet until some man parked his car in the alley garage and came walking past my hideaway, then, much of my naked body got wet as I pressed against the icy ground so he wouldn't see me. This made me seek better shelter since it was about 9 PM—I'd been in the cold an hour—and a whole string of rich bastards with cars might start putting them away. I waited until noon was in sight then dashed down the walk to the alley and leaped up and grabbed the handy drainpipe of a garage and pulled myself up. The win-

dow I'd broken out of overlooked my new
refuge and if anyone went in that bathroom they'd see the havoc wrought in
the place and looking out, see me. This
fear had just formed—I was too cold to
be jolly now—when I saw Mary at last
come into view. She had my pants,
shoes and coat, but not my T-shirt and
socks, having skipped these small items
as she bustled out in front in the cause
of my predicament "straightening up".
The woman had only noticed my belt
and Mary said she had a leather class at
school and was engraving it. When I'd
bashed out the window Mary had heard
the crashing about—the old lady must
have been deaf; while I was escaping
Mary kept talking about Thanksgiving
turkey—and had come into the bathroom to clean up, close the window and
otherwise coverup. I put on my clothes
and chattering uncontrollably from my
freezeout walked with Mary to the "Oasis" for some hot coffee. (This is such a
sick description of this really funny little
scene that I'm almighty sorry that I put

it down. I'm rushing along to complete this letter today and am just careless as hell.) And so it goes, tale after tale revolving around this Cherry Mary period; here's just a couple more: at first the mother of this fucking filly confided in me and, to get me on her side, asked me to take care of Mary, watch her and so forth. After a while, as Mary got wilder, the old bitch decided to give me a dressing down, and since she wasn't the type to do it herself—and to impress me, I guess—she got the pastor of the parish to hand me a lecture. Now, her home was in one of the elite parishes and so she got the monsignor—it was a Catholic church—to come over the same evening she invited me. I arrived a little before him and could at once smell something cooking. The slut just couldn't hold back her little scheme, told Mary to listen closely and began preaching a little of her own gospel to warm me up for the main event. The doorbell rang and her eyes sparkled with anticipation as she sallied forth from the kitchen to answer

it. The priest was a middlesized middleaged pink featured man with extremely thick glasses covering such poor
eyes he couldn't see me until our noses
almost touched. Coming toward me
across the palatial livingroom, he had
his handshake extended and was in the
midst of a normal greeting, the mother
escorting him by elbow all the while and
gushing introduction. Then it happened,
he saw me; what an expression! I've never seen a chin drop so far so fast, it literally banged his breastbone. "Neal! Neal!
my boy!, at last I've found my boy!" His
voice broke as he said the last word and
his adam's apple refused to articulate
further because all it gave out was a
strangled blubber. Choked with emotion,
he violently clasped me to him and flung
his eyes to heaven fervently thanking his
God. Tremendous tears rolled down his
cheeks, poured over his upthrust jaw,
and disappeared inside his clerical collar. I had trouble deciding whether to
leave my arms hanging limp or throw
them around him and try to return the

depth of his feeling with some gesture of my own, I forget just what I did do. But, my goodness, golly and whoooooeee!, what a sight!! The priest's emotion had been one of incredulous joyous recognition, Mary's mother's emotion was a gem of frustrated surprise; startled wonder at such an unimaginable happening left her gaping at us with the most foolish looking face I've ever seen. She didn't know whether to faint or flee, never had she been so taken aback, and I'm sure, didn't think she ever would be, it was really a perfect farce. Mary and her sister—who was there to lend dignity to her mother's idea—were as slackjawed as any of us. Depend on sweet Mary to recover first, she did, with a giggle; which her sister took as a queue to frown upon thereby regaining her senses. The mother's composure came with a gasp of artificial goo, "Well! What a pleasant surprise!!", she gurgled with strained smile. This was as good a coverup as any and I admired her presence of mind, but deplored that she'd snuck out from under so easily. Oho!, but wait, aha!, she made a mistake! Her tension was so unbearable—and she had succeeded so well with her first words—that she decided to speak again, "Let's all go into supper, shall we?" she said in a high-pitched nervous urge. The earnestness of her tone struck us all as most incongruous—and she'd given herself away by being too quick—since her guest was still holding me tightly.

The ecstatic priest was Harlan Schmidt, my Godfather when I was baptized at age 10 in 1936. He had also taught me Latin for some months and saw me occasionally during the following three years I served at Holy Ghost church as an altar boy. At our last meeting I was engrossed in the lives of the Saints and determined to become a priest or Christian brother, then I abruptly disappeared down the pleasanter path of evil. Now, 6 ½ years later, we met again in Mary's house as a youth he'd come to lecture. Well, he didn't get around to the lecture, it never entered

his head because it was too full of bliss-
ful joy at finding his lost son. He told me
how he'd never had another Godson—it
just so happened that way—and how
he'd prayed night and day for my soul
and to see me again. He could hardly contain himself at the dinnertable,
fidgeted and twittered and didn't touch
his food. He dragged the whole story of
his long wait for this moment out into
the open and before the sullen-hearted
(she gave me piercing glances of pure
hate when Father Schmidt wasn't looking) mother actually waxed eloquent.
When the meal was over the dirtyoldbitch knew her sweet little scheme had
backfired completely for Schmidt at once
excused himself, saying he was sure
everyone understood, because he wanted
to talk to me alone, and we left. We drove
to his church and then sat in his car for
two hours before I got out and walked
away, never to see him to this very day,
now five years since. He started in with
the old stuff, and I, knowing there could
be no agreement and not wanting to use

him unfairly, came down right away and
for once I didn't hesitate as I told him
not to bother; I was sorry for it, but we
were worlds apart and it would do not
good for him to try and come closer. Oh
we did a lot of talking, it wasn't quite
that short and simple, but as I say, I
finally left him when he realized there
was nothing more to be said, and that
was that. The other incident I wanted to
tell you about can wait, I must cut this
to the bone from here on out because I
haven't the money for stamps. Anyhow,
the reason for this little glimpse into the
months just prior to meeting Joan was
to show that there was some cause for
what happened to me in the bar with
my younger Blood Brother. Mind you,
I hadn't seen Cherry Mary's mother for
at least a month before this night in the
bar, altho I'd seen Mary about two weeks
earlier. Ah bullshit, what's another
few lines, I gotta break in here and tell
you that other funny little thing about
Cherry Mary. It is this; she was such a
hypochondriac that she often played at

Blindness. Now wait a minute, this was unusual because she never complained of illness or anything else, in fact, she didn't complain about her eyes either, just the opposite, she had a true martyr complex toward them. Often, we'd spend 12-16 hours in a hotel room while she was "blind". I'd wait on her hand and food (and cock) during these times. They'd begin casually enough, she'd simply announce that she couldn't see and that would go on until she'd quietly say she could see again. This happened while she was driving—I'd grab the wheel—while we were walking—I'd lead her—while we were loving—I'd finish—in fact, this happened any old place she felt like it happening. It was a great little game, she didn't have to worry, if she was smackedup in the car, or anything, the old lady would come to the rescue with lots of dough. Oh yes, I forgot, toward the end she began pulling fainting spells and would pass out equally at ease on the street or in a bed; my job at these times was to feel her pulse. Etc.,

etc., I could go on and on about Cherry
Mary, but enough, and back to the exciting story of the loss and downfall of
my one (ahem) pure love. If the gentle (or
otherwise) reader will kindly bear with
me and think back he might remember
that we left our hero snug in his smug
little mind and about to leave a cozy spot
on E. Colfax just before 11PM on Xmas
eve.

Here they came, I knew it before
they'd closed the door behind them, two
big bulls and heading right for me. "Cassady?", they didn't even look at younger
Bloodbrother, must have had a good
description, "come along with us". Presto! I was back in jail again. You've surely guessed by now (if any of this mess
is clear) despite my trying to obtusely
keep it from you. Younger BB had called
CMary, and her mother had arbitrarily
vowed to have me arrested at once, and
Mary, for some perverse reason, helped
her. I was booked for molesting a minor.
Before being led to the tank, (I know the
way by heart from previous trips) I was

brought to the second floor office of a
certain police sergeant. You might recall, Jack, a Mr. Paul J. White who is
a Los Angeles probation officer. I had
four separate rounds with him, I won
the first and third and he came out on
top in the second and last one. Well, I
had the same type of personal duel with
this Denver policeman; not exactly the
same—White was an absolute shit, the
sergeant is just a little fart. Trying to
think of the name of this guy, to write
it down, all I kept coming up with was
Giroux (your editor) but I've finally got
it; this dick's name is Garrard. Now, I
had only two bouts with this jerk, on
the first occasion he'd come off best by
a big margin; did great work, dug up evidence all over the city to put me away
with, here, on the second skirmish, I
beat him, but because he wasn't too unfair and let me do it. Sgt. of detectives
Garrard worked the night shift and was
second in command to Capt. Childers,
who exercised his seniority and worked
days. It was near the bewitching hour

as I was hauled before old Tom Gerrard, a cigar-smoking hard man of 50. He whipped out at me, "where's the money?" I asked him to please come again. "Listen here, you little bastard, I won't take any of your shit, where's the money? I got witnesses that you were in front of the poolhall last night in a car, and when my witness stuck his head inside the car window he saw the moneybag on the floor. Come on now, where's the money?" I swore I didn't know what he was talking about, and dammit, as luck would have it, I'd done exactly the same sort of swearing when I faced him before, only then I *did* know what he was talking about and he proved it. Remembering that last time his voice became grimmer and assumed a more threatening tone. "Now listen, you little son-of-a-bitch, I won't take any more of your lies, so you're just an innocent little punk, huh, well I'm going to have some of the boys work you over and maybe you won't be so dumb when you get back. I'm tired of your lying." At this he got

up and walking to the door, motioned
a big bruiser to come take me away.
By god, this mystery was getting serious and I was scared enough to shit my
pants. "Wait a minute", I pleaded, "I'll
do whatever you say, but I don't know
anything about any money, please explain, honest, I don't know what you're
talking about". We were standing in the
doorway, he hesitated a moment, then,
"Ok", and he went back behind his desk
and I sat before it with the other dick at
my elbow. He told me the poolhall was
robbed last night (the reason I didn't
know about it, although I'd been there
the next day, was because the owners
had shushed it up so everything would
stay normal and give the police a better chance to find out who did it) and
I'd been seen in front of the place after
it closed, in a car with this moneybag
under the seat. This was all true except
the moneybag part, but so were a lot of
other guys and a few cars and this prick
who fingered me for the burglary (money
snatched by forcing the back door) was

full of shit, and just let me face him and prove it. Garrard said he'd see about that and questioned me along these lines, "Do you know a Mary Lou Berle? We got her in a home for expectant mothers, and she put in a complaint a few days ago that you raped her". Jesus Christ—Joan's best friend! How many shocks, happy and otherwise, can a man get in one day? In less than 8 hours I'd been led to Joan, snatched from her, charged with three separate crimes, the first of which wasn't justified, the second one I knew nothing about, and the third a preposterous lie. Think of it! I hadn't even known M.Lou was pregnant, it certainly didn't show thru her fat, and she claimed I did it. Harrumpph! I sure put *that* straight in a hurry, told him I hadn't known her a month ago, she'd just come to town, etc., I think he believed me. The pickup had been put out for me on account of this pool hall business and CMary's mother calling the police had been a happy coincidence that loosened up Garrard enough to let out a chortle over. Finally, with a growl to bust my teeth in if he checked the Poolhall story and found I'd lied, he sent me up-stairs to the lockup.

When a prisoner is released from Colorado State Reformatory he is placed on a year's probation, and if, among other reasons, he is found in a bar his pa-role is revoked and he's sent back to do time and a half. Even if I beat all three of these raps, I'd still have that stick-ler to hurdle. Lying on the inner-steel mattress, I figured my moves in mental shudderings. I had M.Lou whipped at the start, I thought I'd bust the pool-hall thing, too, Cherry Mary might drop charges if I got the priest, Father Schmidt, on the ball. Yep my main worry was parole violation and the only hope to escape that laid on the charity of Sgt. Gerrard.

There is a quality of calm, a collected coolness, a careful restraint that is the foremost feature of the mind when in jail. One is not inclined to rowdiness, the

eyes rove over the cell's fixtures and un-
consciously count each bar. Small things
assume undue importance and nostalgic longing permeates every thought. I
awoke from a night of bad dreams and
was pleased to feel my usual jail-peace
take hold and disperse these phantoms.
A treat was in store, being Christmas
day, the prisoners were allowed the
freedom of the corridor. As on ordinary
days, from 8 to 4 we had the bullpen to
lounge in too. The gospel-army of singers offered 45 minutes diversion by trying to lead the uncooperative jailbirds
in a few Protestant hymns. They offered
to save our souls, using the common
preacher's-voice squeal to give out with
their frantic appeals of foolish logic. This
type of salvation uses many artifices on
its audience, one of the most frequently
presented and most humorous, comes
when the insanely earnest young orator steps forward in his thin-soled black
shoes and shiny conservative black suit
and while peering thru modern attractive glasses tries to fix his victims with

the intense piercing "John Brown", offset with a humble pitiful pleading look,
he always carries a black leather new
testament in his right hand. He would
begin his speech so quietly the uninitiated might take him as a normal person. He sweated to his climax; the voice
rising in progressive chords. He'd work
up to a plateau of minor frenzy, then
drop suddenly to a low drone of imbecilic meekness. Each pitch reached for
a higher wall of platitudes to the Lord
until its embarrassing volume was so
tremendous that the noise of a quick-escape artist sawing thru the bars would
have been easily drowned. The wall-eyed
emphasis he enjoyed best was making
it clear to one and all that he'd sinned
worse than any of them. He thought it
particularly important that everyone
know he was no dumb goodie-goodie. Yessir, he knew what he was yelling
about, before he'd discovered merciful Jesus he had sunk to unspeakable
depths. But, praise the lord and halle-
lujah, the holy spirit had spoken to him

and showed the level of his ways. Just knowing the error of his life, o lordy no, he'd had to accept Jesus into his heart and the erring habits made this a long hard fight. He despaired of ever making heaven until one blessed day he realized he'd been cheating. Horrors and more horrors! (he shuddered violently and squeaked in fear) He'd been cheating the lord, and why?, because he'd kept his pride. It had been a mock surrender to Jesus, he had falsely hidden his pride away like a miser, no sirree, he didn't want to give that up. But, the lord knew it and wouldn't leave him alone until tortured conscience bothered him so there was no longer any way to hold out. Oh, he tried, he sinned right up to the last moment, but it was no use; the lord conquered, as always. What peace when he finally abandoned his soul completely to Jesus!! What joy! What rapture! and he wanted to tell us that nothing could harm him now that Jesus was by his side; he fairly evaporated the steel bars with his hot breath of faith. He blew, no doubt about that, he blew to exhaustion and when he gave up he knew he'd failed to stir us, the cage was still there unmolested; each had his own. Stepping back into his group's lineup, sadness that this fact touched only his lips, the rest of his visible self regained the composure of a bank clerk. The next to preach to us was the lone young girl from out of the three or four old women and several men stretched so prim along the bars; the very bars thru which a sick Mexican had puked his mush. They stood, too, beside the cell where, a few hours before, a poor white guy had given up his ghost to acute alcoholism; I heard his moaning all night and thought him just ordinarily ill from drink. They found him dead at morning checkup. (The services are closed, the sermon's over. I was going to give a nice nasty sketch of a sweet twat urging us villains to join her in Christ. But no, the idea of that old man expiring in the adjoining cell, with his cries unanswered, has unnerved me so I can't get sexy. The tale continues.)

The City and County of Denver didn't provide me with the feast I'd anticipated from Joan's generous couple. The poor food was partially made up for by a semi-precious treasure—I found a song-and-dance man in jail. His name I've forgotten but not his looks. He was a near-perfect replica of Danny Kaye and patterned his patter after him; this 5 years ago too, when Kaye was just getting in bigtime. He was really very funny and never at loss for a quip; I'll modify this because being the only entertainment in sight his antics were hungrily picked up by me without criticism, besides I favored his clowning since I'd known a similar fool named John Chevrolotti in L.A. in 1942. Quick with the wit from having worked the nightclubs all over the U.S.A., this D.Kaye also had many crazy charades of prominent people to toss at me. We became jailpals and he told me some crazy slut stuck up a place and he'd been living with her and the cops had him for questioning. Bemoaning the fact that he'd lost a good

job and fallen to the level of a jailbird,
he put on such a hilarious show I split
with laughter. Summarizing him quickly,
I say he so enlivened the place with his
comic tragedy that I scarcely had time
for any morbid brooding or serious planning.

But the time for serious thoughts had
come, Garrard called me to his office
the day before New Year's, 1946. I tried
to ready a spiel to rival the only speech
I'm proud of—my talk escape from San
Quentin in 1944—yet knew I didn't have
it as I came before his ugly face. Oh joy,
oh happy day, oh unbelievably pretty words. He said I was free!—not now
tho, to teach me a little "respect", as he
put it. I was to stay in jail until Jan. 2nd
and miss any NY celebration. That was
alright with me, I poured out thanks because I knew he was being good enough
to forget about the parole violation. After
all, he could have sent me up for a minimum of 18 months. He had said earlier
he would, if he took a mind to, whether
the poolhall story checked out or not.

Evidently it did check out for he didn't
mention it. His flatfeet told him what an
obvious whore Mary Lou Berle was, so
he gave me the benefit of the doubt there
and Cherry Mary's mother had dropped
her charge on Xmas day, just teaching
me a lesson, she told him. (I remember
now a big lecture—and this is highly unusual for Garrard—he gave it to me on
ruining a fine girl from a good family like
Cherry Mary's.) So I was free, yippee! I
went back upstairs bubbling.

One other thing I did in that jail, and
that was very easy to do considering
my exultant condition. I vowed never to
be in jail again. I'd done this before of
course, but I mention it here only because I never have. And perhaps I might
be allowed to say that this final vow I
somehow knew would be kept, although
I suspect—as would anyone else—I think
now that I felt that way then only in the
light of the subsequent events, i.e., I've
been prison-free ever since. (Hastily I
add that nowadays I don't feel the security of this vow being upheld and tho I

certainly won't commit any overt act to land behind bars, Allen's Chance might pop up.)

I left jail for the last time on January 2nd at 9 AM. I went to the poolhall and bummed breakfast and a shave. I hurried from the barbershop to 162 Lincoln St. My sweet dove had fled, the lady said Joan had waited 3 days for me to return and then went to Ft. Collins. Woe for me, I went back to the poolhall. (Listen Jack, I've just gotten a chance for one more trip on RR, although I've been cut off for a week, so since I've got to leave SF within the hour will rush this off to you.) I went to Ed Uhl's ranch, you recall my letters of nonsense to Haldon, I wrote others to Brierly too. I came back to Denver to pick up a cow for old man Uhl, I was to stay overnight and get the bull (I think it was a bull) back next day. I ran into J.Holmes, he knew where Joan was, I flipped, I found her. I can't possibly describe that night, I know I intended to fill up 10 pages with the description of it. Suffice to say here that she had been back in Denver since April (early) and it was the Ides of May (I'm not confused) where we had our 8 hours together. She was a whore, I mean she was living as a whore from one man to another. Paradoxically, her virginal nature was more pronounced than ever—she asked to kiss my privates—even tho she had learned to make love mechanically like a whore. I haven't seen her since. But enuf, The End.

I got the letter from Rambler (that's you) and Moe (Johnny boy) and I didn't say, or didn't intend, "Now that I got Jack married off—" etc, I meant now that Jack is married, I wouldn't be surprised, or next in line—Allen and Anso. Here's the horror: you mean you didn't get a letter from me about Dec.7th? I wrote a big typewritten one, too; Now Honourable Married Man and thought you'd surely get it, so put no name on it—dammit—these extra mailment on Xmas much can't read.

Give love—altho I'm sure she won't

want it if she accidently reads any of this—to your wife and Merry Xmas to your mother I also sent this letter to Allen G. but lost his address and guessed it to be 416E. 34th St. Paterson, N.J., right? I sent Allen's letter off at Thanksgiving, if you see him ask if he got it. Neither of these two letters have returned here, so let me know, huh?

NEAL CASSADY - TIMELINE

February 8, 1926. Born Neal Leon Cassady in Salt Lake City, Utah. Parents Maud (sometimes Maude) Webb (nickname Jean) Scheur and Neal Marshall Cassady. Mother previously married to James Kenneth Daly, lawyer of Sioux City, Iowa, with whom she had eight children. Marries Neal Sr. in 1925. Neal born a year later. Mother dies of pneumonia in 1936.

1932. Mother moves out, leaving Neal with father.

1930s. Depression-era childhood flophouse and street life with his father, barber, alcoholic, and frequent itinerant and jailee, in Denver.

1933. Hobo trip with father to Utah, New Mexico and California.

1940-1944. Beginning at age 14 and until 18 and beyond steals on his own reckoning 500 or so cars. Joyriding. Three arrests.

1940. Sent to Mullen Homes for Boys but absconds.

1942. Summer in Los Angeles. Suspected robbery charge but released.

1943. Sent to California Juvenile Forestry Camp after charges of joyriding.

1944. Arrested for stolen goods and sent to Colorado State Reformatory. Intensive reading.

1945. Birth of son Robert William Hyatt Jr. by Maxine Beam. Affair with JOAN ANDERSON.

August, 1946. Marries 16-year-old LuAnne Henderson in Denver.

1946-7. Meetings with Jack Kerouac in New York City through Hal Chase, a Columbia University student also from Denver, the beginning of a lifelong relationship and correspondence. Also begins relationship with Ginsberg.

March 1947. Returns to Denver from New York. Meets Carolyn Cassady, née Robinson, Bennington College graduate and graduate student in Fine Arts and Theatre at the University of Denver. Start of extensive letter-writing to Ginsberg and Kerouac.

1947. Visits William Burroughs' marijuana and citrus farm in New Waverly, Texas with Ginsberg and where Herbert Huncke is living.

1940-50s. Works intermittently as a railroad brakeman for the Southern Pacific Railroad.

April 1, 1948. Carolyn and Neal marry after annulment of Neal's marriage to LuAnne Henderson.

September 7, 1948. Birth of Cathleen Joanne Cassady.

Winter, 1948. Visits Kerouac then staying with his sister in Rocky Mount, North Carolina.

1948. Begins writing the autobiography that will become *The First Third.*

1949. Travels cross-country to New York with Kerouac.

1950. Bigamously marries Diana Hansen, mother of their child Curtis Hansen, born 1950.

January 26 , 1950. Birth of Melany Jane Cassady.

December, 1950. Writes the Joan Anderson letter to Jack Kerouac.

September 9, 1951. Birth of John Allen Cassady.

December, 1951/January, 1952. Arrival and stay of Jack Kerouac in the San Francisco household and *ménage-à-trois* as *On The Road* is being revised and rewritten.

1952. Cassady family moves to San José.

April, 1953. Breaks his leg in a Southern Pacific Railroad shunting accident. In March 1954 the railway settles for $16,000.

August, 1954. He and Carolyn buy house in Los Gatos close to the Santa Cruz mountains with the accident insurance money. Attempts to rewrite his autobiography. Loses $10,000 dollars of their investment money, fraudulently withdrawn, in racetrack horse gambling, long an obsession.

October 7, 1955. Attends the historic 6 Gallery reading, San Francisco, organized by Kenneth Rexroth. Ginsberg reads "Howl." Also reading are Philip Lamantia, Michael McClure, Gary Snyder and Philip Whalen. Lawrence Ferlinghetti, Jack Kerouac, Peter Orlovsky and Ann Charters present.

December, 1955. Suicide of Cassady's lover Natalie Jackson in San Francisco.

1956. Allen Ginsberg dedicates *Howl and Other Poems* to Kerouac, Burroughs and Cassady. "Howl" invokes Cassady as "N.C., secret hero of these poems."

1957. Publication of Kerouac's *On The Road.* The figure of Dean Moriarty based on Cassady.

February, 1958. Arrested for marijuana sale to undercover agent in San Francisco. Serves two years of five in San Quentin State Prison, Marin County.

June, 1960. Released from prison. Parole for three years.

1961. Begins affair with Anne Murphy.

1962. Meets up with Ken Kesey and the Merry Pranksters.

1963. Divorce of Carolyn and Neal Cassady.

1963. Lives briefly, along with Allen Ginsberg, at the Haight Ashbury apartment of the poet-publisher and filmmaker Charles Plymell.

1964.   Drives Ken Kesey's Merry Pranksters Harvester School Bus (named
Further) from San Francisco to New
York. He and Kesey take copious LSD.
See Tom Wolfe, *The Electric Cool-Aid
Acid Test* (1968) and the movie *Magic
Trip* (2011), Dir. Alex Gibney. Cassady
wanted by the law. Also the memoir
of his partner Anne Murphy, *Tripping
with a Viper*, excerpted in *Sparring
with Beatnik Ghosts* (2012).

1965.   Stays with Kesey in La Honda.

December 3, 1966. Carolyn throws farewell
party for Neal on eve of his departure
for Mexico but he is drugged and
psychotic.

January, 1967. Travels to Puerto Vallarta,
Jalisco, Mexico, with Anne Murphy
and fellow Prankster George Walker.
Affair with Janice Brown and shared
travel across America.

February 4, 1968. Death aged 41 in San Mi-
guel de Allende, Guanajuato, Mexico.
Found unconscious by the railroad
tracks. Generally thought to have
mixed drugs and alcohol though cause
of death listed as "general congestion."

October 21, 1969. Death of Jack Kerouac

1971. Publication of *The First Third* by City Lights.

1972. Kerouac's estate publishes *Visions of Cody* as a tribute novel to Cassady in the person of Cody Pomeray.

1978. Publication of *As Ever: The Collected Correspondence of Allen Ginsberg and Neal Cassady.*

1980. Movie *Heart Beat.* Dir. John Byrum. Based on Carolyn Cassady, *Heart Beat: My Life with Jack & Neal,* 1976.

1981. Publication of revised and expanded *The First Third and Other Writings.*

1990. Publication of Carolyn Cassady, *Off the Road: My Years with Cassady, Kerouac, and Ginsberg.*

1997. Movie. *The Last Time I Committed Suicide.* Dir. Stephen T. Kay. Based on the Joan Anderson letter.

April 5, 1997. Death of Allen Ginsberg.

2001. Swedish film documentary (English language), *Love Always, Carolyn,* Dir. Malin Korkeasalo and Maria Ramström.

2004. Publication of *Neal Cassady: Collected Letters, 1944-1967.*

November 14, 2014. "Neal Cassady's 'Joan Anderson Letter' Found," Web. *Kerouac.com.* Jerry Cimino, The Beat Museum.

December 16, 2014. "Reconsidering the Importance of the Joan Anderson Letter," Web. David S. Wills, *Beatdom.*

February 9, 2017. "Joan Anderson Letter Goes to Auction... Again," Web. David S. Wills, *Beatdom.*

February 10, 2017. "The Joan Anderson Letter," Web. *The Allen Ginsberg Project.*

March 8, 2017. "The Joan Anderson Letter," auctioned by Heritage Auctions.

September 2017. Purchase of the Joan Anderson letter by Emory University, Georgia for the Stuart A. Rose Manuscript, Archives and Rare Book Library. On view September 2017-May 2018 as part of the public exhibition titled "The Dream Machine: The Beat Generation and Counterculture 1945-1975."

SELECTIVE BIBLIOGRAPHY
Neal Cassady

The First Third, A Partial Autobiography, and Other Writings, San Francisco: City Lights Books, 1971.

As Ever: The Collected Correspondence of Allen Ginsberg and Neal Cassady, Foreword by Carolyn Cassady, Berkeley: Creative Arts Book Company, 1977.

The First Third, A Partial Autobiography & Other Writings, Revised and Expanded Edition Together with a New Prologue, eds. Ed McClanahan, Ken Babbs, San Francisco; City Lights Books, 1981.

Grace Beats Karma: Letters from Prison 1958-1960, New York: Blast Books, 1993.

O Fatal Practicality: The Surviving Portion of the Joan Anderson Letter, Louisville: Contre Coup Press, 2014.

Neal Cassady: Collected Letters, 1944-1967, ed. David Moore, New York Penguin, 2004.

Excerpts from Visions of Neal: A Boy's Life with his Father. Chapters three and four: Neal's Wheel Karma, San Francisco: Beat Museum Press, 2007.

Criticism, Biography, Memoir

Berrigan, Ted, "Jack Kerouac: The Art of Fiction," Interview, *Paris Review, 41,* Issue 43, Summer 1968. Reprinted Kevin Jackson, ed. *Conversations with Jack Kerouac,* Jackson, Mississippi: University Press of Mississippi, 2005.

Cassady, Carolyn, Vimeo. "Telephone interview with Carolyn Cassady, wife of Neal Cassady." Recorded April18, 2002, with Kurt Hemmer and students, Harper College, Palatine, Ohio.

────── *Off The Road: My Life with Jack & Neal,* New York: William Morrow, 1990, New York: Penguin, 1991.

────── *Heart Beat: My Life with Jack & Neal,* Berkeley: Creative Arts Book Company, 1976.

Dardess, George, "The Logic of Spontaneity: A Reconsideration of Kerouac's 'Spontaneous Prose Method,'" *boundary*, 2, 3:3, Spring, 1975, 729-46.

Deakin, Richard, *Jack and Neal, Angels Still Falling: The Story of Kerouac and Cassady, A Play*, Warwickshire: Beat Scene Press, 1997.

The Last Time I Committed Suicide. Dir. Stephen Kay. Movie based on the incidents described in the Joan Anderson Letter, 1997.

Dunham, Greg, *Speed Limit, A One-Man Show in Two Acts, Based on the Life and Writings of Neal Cassady*, Toronto: Playwright's Union of Canada, 1985.

Kesey, Ken, *The Day After Superman Died*, Northridge, California: Lord John Press, 1980.

Kopp, Zack, *The Denver Beat Scene: The Mile-High Legacy of Kerouac, Cassady and Ginsberg*, Charleston, South Carolina: The History Press, 2015.

Neal Cassady, Biopic. Dir. Noah Buschel, 2007.

Nicosia, Gerald, *One and Only: The Untold Story of On The Road and Luanne Henderson, the Woman Who Started Jack Kerouac and Neal Cassady on Their Journey,* New York: Cleis Press, 2013.

Plummer, William, *The Holy Goof: A Biography of Neal Cassady,* New York: Paragon House, 1981.

Sandison, David, and Vickers, Graham, *Neal Cassady: The Fast Life of a Beat Hero,* Chicago: Chicago Review Press, 2006, Omnibus Press, 2010.

Spit in the Ocean, No. 6, "The Cassady Issue," Pleasant Hill, Oregon; 1981.

Staton, Scott, "Neal Cassady: American 'Muse, Holy Fool," *The New Yorker Magazine,* December 12, 2012.

Tallman, Warren, "Kerouac's Sound," *The Tamarack Review*, 11, 1959. 58-74.

Jack Kerouac

The Town and The City, New York: Harcourt Brace, 1950.

On The Road, New York: Viking, 1957.

The Dharma Bums, New York: Viking, 1958.

The Subterraneans, New York: Grove Press, 1958

Doctor Sax: Faust Part Three, New York: Grove Press, 1959.

Maggie Cassidy: A Love Story, New York: Avon, 1959.

Mexico City Blues, New York: Grove Press, 1960.

Lonesome Traveler, New York: McGraw Hill, 1960.

The Scripture of the Golden Eternity, Chevy Chase: Totem Press/Corinth, 1960.

Tristessa, New York: Avon, 1960.

Book of Dreams, San Francisco: City Lights Books, 1961.

Pull My Daisy, New York: Grove Press, 1961.

Big Sur, New York: Farrar, Straus, 1962.

Desolation Angels, New York: Coward-McCann, 1965.

Satori in Paris, New York: Grove Press, 1966.

Vanity of Duluoz: An Adventurous Education, 1935-1946, New York: Coward, 1968.

Pic, New York: Grove Press, 1971.

Scattered Poems, San Francisco: City Lights Books, 1971.

Visions of Cody, New York: McGraw-Hill, 1972.

Pomes All Sizes, San Francisco: City Lights Books, 1992.

Good Blonde & Others, San Francisco: Grey Fox Press, 1993, 2001.

Old Angel Midnight, San Francisco: Grey Fox, 1993.

Book of Blues, New York: Penguin, 1995.

The Portable Jack Kerouac, ed. Ann Charters. New York: Viking, 1995.

Jack Kerouac: Selected Letters, 1940–1956 ed. Ann Charters. New York: Viking, 1995.

Book of Haikus, New York: Penguin, 2003.

Windblown World: The Journals of Jack Kerouac 1947-1954, ed. Douglas Brinkley, New York: Viking, 2004.

Road Novels 1957–1960, *On The Road*, *The Dharma Bums*, *The Subterraneans*, *Tristessa*, *Lonesome Traveler*, New York: Library of America, 2007.

On The Road: The Original Scroll, ed. Howard Cunnell, New York: Viking, 2007.

And The Hippos Were Boiled in Their Tanks,
     with William Burroughs, New York:
     Grove Press, 1945, 2008.

On The Road: The Original Scroll, New York:
     Penguin Classics, 2008.

The Sea is My Brother, New York: Penguin,
     1942, 2011.

The Haunted Life and Other Writings, ed.
     Todd Tietchen, Boston: DaCapo,
     2014.

Criticism, Biography

Amburn, Ellis, *Subterranean Kerouac:*
     The Hidden Life of Jack Kerouac,
     New York: St. Martin's Press, 1998.

Amram, David, *Offbeat: Collaborating*
     with Kerouac, New York: Thunder's
     Mouth, 2002.

Beaulieu, Victor-Lévy (1972), *Jack Kerouac:*
     Essai Poulet, Editions du Jour,
     1972.

     Trans *Jack Kerouac: A Chicken Es-*
     say, Toronto: Coach House, 1975.

Charters, Ann, *Kerouac: A Biography*, San
     Francisco: Straight Arrow Books,
     1973.

———— *A Bibliography of The Works of Jack Kerouac*, New York: Phoenix, 1973.

Charters, Ann, and Charters, Sam, *Brother-Souls, John Clellon Holmes, Jack Kerouac and the Beat Generation*, Jackson: University Press of Mississippi, 2010.

Clark, Tom, *Jack Kerouac*, New York: Harcourt Brace Jovanovich, 1984. Donaldson, Scott, ed. *On The Road: Text and Criticism*, New York: Viking, 1979.

Ellis, R.J., *Liar! Liar! Jack Kerouac, Novelist*, London: Greenwich Exchange, 1999.

French, Warren, *Jack Kerouac: Novelist of the Beat Generation*, Boston: Twayne, 1986.

García-Robles, Jorge, *At The End of the Road: Jack Kerouac in Mexico*, Trans. Daniel C. Schechter, Minneapolis: University of Minnesota Press, 2014.

Gifford, Barry, and Lee, Lawrence, *Jack's Book: An Oral Biography of Jack Kerouac*, New York: St. Martin's Press, 1978.

Grace, Nancy M., *Jack Kerouac and the Literary Imagination*, New York: Palgrave, 2007.

Hipkiss, Robert A., *Jack Kerouac: Prophet of the New Romanticism*, Lawrence: The Regents Press of Kansas, 1976.

Holmes, John Clellon, *Gone in October: Last Reflections on Jack Kerouac*, Hailey: Limberlost Press, 1985.

Holladay, Hilary and Holton, Robert, eds. *What's Your Road Man? Critical Essays on Jack Kerouac's On The Road*, Carbondale: University of Southern Illinois Press, 2009.

Holton, Robert, *On The Road: Kerouac's Ragged American Journey*, New York: Twayne, 1999.

Hrebeniak, Michael, *Action Writing: Jack Kerouac's Wild Form*, Carbondale: Southern Illinois University Press, 2006.

Hunt, Tim, *The Textuality of Soulwork; Jack Kerouac's Quest for Spontaneous Prose*, Ann Arbor: University of Michigan Press, 2014.

——— *Kerouac's Crooked Road: Development of a Fiction*, Hamden: Archon, 1981.

Jarvis, Charles E., *Visions of Kerouac: A Biography*, Lowell: Ithaca Press., 1974.

Johnson, Joyce, *The Voice is All: The Lonely Victory of Jack Kerouac*, New York: Viking, 2012.

Jones, James T., *A Map of Mexico City Blues*, Carbondale: University of Southern Illinois Press, 2010.

―――― *Use My Name: Jack Kerouac's Forgotten Families*, Ontario: ECW Press, 1999.

―――― *Jack Kerouac's Duluoz Legend: The Mythic Form of an Autobiographical Fiction*, Carbondale: Southern Illinois University Press, 1999.

Maher, Paul, ed. *Empty Phantoms: Interviews and Encounters with Jack Kerouac*, New York: Thunder's Mouth Press, 2005.

―――― *Kerouac: The Definitive Biography*, New York: Taylor Trade, 2004.

McNally, Dennis, *Desolate Angel: Jack Kerouac, The Beats, and America*, New York: Random House, 1979.

Melehy, Hassan, *Kerouac: Language, Poetics, and Territory*, New York and London: Bloomsbury Academic, 2016.

Miles, Barry, *Jack Kerouac: King of the Beats*, New York: Henry Holt, 1998.

Nicosia, Gerald, *Kerouac: The Last Quarter-Century*, Corte Madera, California: Noodlebrain Press, 2019.

———— *Memory Babe: A Critical Biography of Jack Kerouac*, New York; Grove Press, 1983, Berkeley: University of California Press, 1994.

Poteet, Maurice, *Textes de l'Exode*, Montréal: Guerin literature, 1987.

Ring, Kevin, *All Day Looking for His Hat...: Essays on Jack Kerouac and Other Stories*, Ziri: Editions Baes, 2014.

Swartz, Omar, *The View from* On The Road: *The Rhetorical Vision of Jack Kerouac*, Carbondale: Southern Illinois University Press. 1999.

Theado, Matt, *Understanding Jack Kerouac*, Columbia: University of South Carolina Press, 2000.

Turner, Steve, *Angel-Headed Hipster*, London: Bloomsbury, 1996.

Weaver, Helen, *The Awakener: A Memoir of Kerouac and the Fifties*, San Francisco: City Lights, 2009.

Weinreich, Regina, *The Spontaneous Poetics of Jack Kerouac: A Study of the Fiction*, Carbondale: Southern Illinois University Press, 1987.

Selected Beat Studies

Adler, Edwards, and Mindich, Bernards, eds. *Beat Art: Visual Works by or about the Beat Generation*, New York: New York School of Education, 1994.

Allen, Donald, and Tallman, Warren, *The Poetics of the New American Poetry*, New York: Grove Press, 1973.

Ash, Mel, *Beat Spirit; The Way of the Beat Writer as a Living Experience*, New York: Penguin Putnam, 1997.

Asher, Levi, ed. *Beats in Time: A Literary Generation's Legacy*, New York: Literary Kicks, 2011.

Bartlett, Jeffery, *One Vast Page: Essays on the Beat Writers, Their Books, and My Life, 1950–1980*, Berkeley: J. Bartlett, 1991.

Bartlett, Lee, ed. *The Beats: Essays in Criticism*, North Carolina: McFarland, 1981.

Beckett, Larry, *Beat Poetry*, St. Andrews: Beatdom, 2012.

Belletto, Steven, *The Beats: A Literary History*, New York: Cambridge University Press, 2020.

———— ed. *The Cambridge Companion to the Beats*, New York: Cambridge University Press, 2017.

Bockris, Victor, *Beat Punks*, Boston: Da Capo, 1998.

Brossard, Chandler, ed. *The Scene Before You: A New Approach to American Culture*, New York: Rinehart & Co, 1955.

Briggs, Robert, *Ruined Time: The 1950s and The Beat*, Scappoose: RBA Publishing, 2006.

Burns, Jim, *Rebels, Beats and Poets*, Penniless Publications, online, 2015.

Campbell, James, *This is the Beat Generation: New York-San Francisco-Paris*, Berkeley: University of California Press, 1999.

Carr, Roy, *The Hip: Hipsters, Jazz and The Beat Generation*, London: Faber, 1986.

Charters, Ann, ed. *Beat Down to Your Soul: What was the Beat Generation?*, New York: Penguin Books, 2001.

—— *Beats and Company: A Portrait of a Literary Generation*, Garden City: Doubleday, 1986.

Cherkovski, Neeli, *Whitman's Wild Children*, Venice: Lapis Press, 1988.

Clay, Steven. and Philips, Rodney, *A Secret Location on the Lower East Side: Adventures in Writing, 1960–1980*, New York: The New York Public Library and Granary Books, 1989.

Cook, Bruce, *The Beat Generation: The Tumultuous '50s Movement and Impact on Today*, New York: Scribner's, 1971.

Cottrell, Robert C., *Sex, Drugs, and Rock 'n' Roll: The Rise of America's 1960s Counterculture*, Lanham: Rowman & Littlefield, 2015.

Damon, Maria, *The Dark End of the Street*, Minneapolis: Minnesota University Press, 1993.

Elkholy, Sharyn, ed. *The Philosophy of the Beats*, Lexington: The University Press of Kentucky, 2012.

Fazzino, Jimmy, *World Beats: Beat Generation Writing and the Worldling of U.S. Writing*, Dartmouth: University Press of New England, 2016.

Foster, Edward Halsey, *Understanding the Beats*, Columbia: University of South Carolina Press, 1992.

Gair, Christopher, *The Beat Generation: A Beginner's Guide*, Oxford: Oneworld, 2008.

Geis, Deborah, ed. *Beat Drama: Playwright and Performances of the "Howl" Generation*, London: Bloomsbury, 2016.

Grace, Nancy M. and Skerl, Jennie, eds. *The Transnational Beat Generation*, New York: Palgrave, 2012.

Halberstam, David, *The Fifties*, New York: Villard Books, 1993.

Harris, Oliver, and McKay, Polina, ed, *Global Beat Studies, Comparative Literature and Culture* (GLC, 2017), On-line.

Horemans, Rudi, ed. *Beat Indeed!*, Antwerp: EXA, 1985.

Knight, Brenda, *Women of the Beat Generation*, San Francisco: Conari Books, 1996.

Lardas, John, *The Bop Apocalypse: The Religious Visions of Kerouac, Ginsberg, and Burroughs*, Urbana: University of Illinois Press, 2001.

—— ed. *Beat Culture, Icons, Lifestyles, and Impact*, Santa Barbara: ABC-CLIO, 2005.

Lee, A. Robert, ed. *The Beat Generation Writers*, London: Pluto Press, 1996.

—— *Designs of Blackness: Mappings in the Literature and Culture of Afro-America*, London: Pluto Press, 1998.

—— *Modern American Counter Writing: Beats, Outriders, Ethnics*, New York: Routledge, 2010.

—— ed. *The Routledge Handbook of International Beat Literature*, New York: Routledge, 2018.

—— *The Beats: Authorships, Legacies*, Edinburgh: Edinburgh University Press, 2019.

Lipton, Lawrence, *The Holy Barbarians*, New York: Messner, 1959.

Marler, Regina, *Queer Beats: How the Beats Turned on America*, Berkeley: Cleis Press, 2004.

Martinez, Manuel Luis, *Countering the Counterculture: Rereading Postwar American Dissent from Jack Kerouac to Tomás Rivera*, Madison: University of Wisconsin Press, 2003.

Maynard, John A., *Venice West: The Beat Generation in Southern California*, New Brunswick, NJ: Rutgers University Press, 1991.

McDarrah, Fred W., *Kerouac and Friends: A Beat Generation Album*, New York: William Morrow, 1986.

McDarrah, Fred W., and McDarrah, Gloria, *Beat Generation: Glory Days in Greenwich Village*, New York: Schirmer Books, 1996.

Miles, Barry, *The Beat Hotel: Ginsberg, Burroughs, and Corso in Paris, 1958-1963*, New York; Grove Press, 2000.

Miller, Douglas T., and Nowak, Marion, *The Fifties: The Way We Really Were*, New York: Doubleday, 1977.

Morgan, Bill, *The Best Minds of My Generation: A Literary History of the Beats*, New York: Grove Press, 2017.

—— *Beat Atlas: A Guide to the Beat Generation in America*, San Francisco: City Lights Books, 2011.

———— *The Typewriter is Holy: The Complete, Uncensored History of the Beat Generation*, New York: Free Press, 2010.

———— *The Beat Generation in San Francisco: A Literary Tour*, San Francisco: City Lights Books, 2003.

———— *The Beat Generation in New York: A Walking Tour of Jack Kerouac's City*, San Francisco; City Lights Books, 1997.

Mortenson, Erik, *Capturing The Beat Moment: Cultural Politics and the Poetics of Presence*, Carbondale: Southern Illinois University Press, 2010.

Myrsiades, Kostas, ed. *The Beat Generation: Critical Essays*, New York: Peter Lang, 2002.

Neville, Richard, *Hippie, Hippie shake: the Dreams, the trips, the trials, the love-ins, the screw-ups...the Sixties*, London: Bloomsbury, 1995.

Newhouse, Thomas, *The Beat Generation and the Popular Novel in the United States, 1945-1970*, Jefferson; MacFarland, 2000.

Pantano, Patricia A., *Women of the Beat Generation, Joyce Johnson, Diane di Prima, and Carolyn Cassady: Female Agency in Transitional Times*, Ann Arbor: ProQuest, 2010.

Podhoretz, Norman, *Doings and Undoings: The Fifties and After in American Writing*, New York: Farrar, Straus and Company, 1964.

Polsky, Ned, *Beats, Hustlers, and Others*, New York: Doubleday, 1967.

Prince, Michael, *Adapting The Beat Poets: Burroughs, Ginsberg and Kerouac on Screen*, Lanham, Maryland: Rowman & Littlefield, 2016.

Rosen, Ralph and Murnaghan, Sheila, *The Hip Sublime: Beat Writers and the Classical Tradition*, Columbus: Ohio State University Press, 2017.

Sargent, Jack, *Naked Lens: An Illustrated History of Beat Cinema*, London: Creation Books, 1997.

Skerl, Jennie, ed. *Teaching Beat Literature*, *College Literature* Special Issue, 27:1,Winter, 2000.

——— ed. *Reconstructing The Beats*, New York: Palgrave, 2000.

Stefanelli, Maria Anita, ed. *City Lights: Pocket Poets and Pocket Books*, Rome: Ila Palma, Mazzone Editori, 2004.

Sterritt, David, *The Beats: A Very Short Introduction*, New York: Oxford University Press, 2013.

—— *Screening the Beats: Media Culture and the Beat Sensibility*, Carbondale: Southern Illinois University Press; 2004.

—— *Mad To be Saved: The Beats, the '50s, and Film*, Carbondale: Southern Illinois University Press, 1998.

Stevenson, Gregory, *The Daybreak Boys: Essays on the Literature of the Beat Generation*, Carbondale: Southern Illinois University Press, 1990.

—— *Pilgrims to Elsewhere: Reflections on Writings by Jack Kerouac, Allen Ginsberg, Gregory Corso, Bob Kaufman and Others*, Roskilde: Eyecorner Press, 2013.

Strausbaugh, Joseph, *The Village: 400 Years of Beats and Bohemians, Radicals and Rogues, A History of Greenwich Village*, New York: Ecco/HarperCollins, 2013.

Sukenick, Ronald, *Down and In: Life in the Underground*, New York: Collier, 1987.

Tietchen, Todd F., *The Cubalogues: Beat Writers in Revolutionary Cuba* Gainesville: University Press of Florida, 2010.

Tonkinson, Carol, ed. *Big Sky Mind: Buddhism and the Beat Generation* New York: Riverhead, 1995.

Tytell, John, *Beat Transnationalism*, Beatdom Books, 2017.

—— *The Beat Interviews*, Beatdom Books, 2014.

—— *Writing Beat and Other Occasions of Literary Mayhem*, Nashville: Vanderbilt University Press, 2014.

—— *Paradise Outlaws: Remembering The Beats*, New York: William Morrow, 1999.

—— *Naked Angels: The Lives and the Literature of the Beat Generation* New York: McGraw-Hill, 1976.

Van Minnen, Cornelis, Van der Bent, Jaap, and Van Elteren, eds. *Beat Culture: The 1950s and Beyond*, Amsterdam: VU University Press, 1999.

Warner, Simon, *Text and Drugs and Rock 'n' Roll: The Beats and Rock Culture*, London: Bloomsbury, 2013.

Watson, Steven, *The Birth of the Beat Generation: Visionaries, Rebels, and Hipsters, 1944-1960*, New York: Pantheon Books, 1995.

Whaley, Preston, *Blows Like a Horn: Beat Writing, Jazz, Style, and Markets in the Transformation of US Culture*, Cambridge, Massachusetts: Harvard University Press, 2004.

Whaley-Bridge, John, *The Emergence of Buddhist American Literature*, Albany: SUNY Press, 2009.

Wilentz, Elias, *The Beat Scene*, New York: Corinth, 1960.

Reference

Charters, Ann, ed. *The Beats: Literary Bohemians in Postwar America* Dictionary of Literary Biography, Vol. 16, Detroit: Gale Research Co, 1983.

Hemmer, Kurt, ed. *Encyclopedia of Beat Literature*, New York: Facts on File, 2007.

Hickey, Morgan, *Bohemian Register: An Annotated Bibliography of the Beat Literary Movement*, Metuchen, NJ: Scarecrow Press, 1990.

Lawlor, William, *The Beat Generation: A Bibliographic Teaching Guide* Lanham: Scarecrow Press, 1998.

Morgan, Bill, *The Beats Abroad: A Global Guide to the Beat Generation* San Francisco: City Lights Books, 2015.

Pekar, Harvey, *The Beats: A Graphic History*, San Francisco: City Lights Books, 2009.

Phillips, Lisa, ed. *Beat Culture and the New America: 1958-1965*, New York: Whitney Museum of American Art/ Flammarion, 1996.

Theado, Matt, ed. *The Beats: A Literary Reference*, New York: Carroll & Graff, 2001.

Varner, Paul, *Historical Dictionary of the Beat Movement* Lanham: Scarecrow Press, 2012.

Weldman, Rich, *The Beat Generation FAQ*, Milwaukee; Beatback Books, 2015.

THE JOAN ANDERSON LETTER

Dear Jack;   Dec, 17,50

   To hell with the dirty lousy shit, I've had enough horseshit.
I got my own pure little bangtail mind and the confines of its binding
please me yet. I wake to more horrors than Céline, not a vain statement
for now I've passed thru just repititious shudderings and nightmare twitches.
I have discovered new sure doom, but this is my secret, and if I'm to find
the pleasure of its devulgance in recognizable form I must tighten my grip
while abiding the wait of years. The exquisite twists of this self-wrought
terror rival Fleur de Mal in that they are as hopeless. Aha! I am well
beyond hope, though, and my helplessness has only tiny Action to dominate.
I am fettered by cobwebs, countless fine creases indelibly etched on the brai
There are no unexplored paths in my mind and few that are not entangled in
the weave of my misery mists. It is but gentle fog thru which I navigate
and make friendly by constant intimate communion. Within the hour from
arising off the suffer-couch each sleep I've gained anew the daily greasefor
and the bearings on which I roll. I embrace to its exhaustion the night's
gleanings with the sure calm mind now mantained by my dry brittle soul.
This calls for strength, you bums, all jump off the gravy-train of stupidity.
Fall to the game of your inheritance and shove to the hilt for salvation.
I'm within my rights, for deep are the roots and deeper its norishment.
Lovely Life, where is thy sting?
   Dark facts I put to you; I've been cut off. I had to go to San Luis O.
for the last 10 days. I earned but 180 bucks in last 5 weeks. The fixing
of the car for east trip is proving well nigh impossible. If I must travel
by train, transportation of tape recorder big problem, but on the soul of
death I vow to have you and this fragile instrument wedded within the month.
I must tomorrow find job here in SF to get money for trip. Carolyn is about
to starve, as is Diana. Poverty looms big, to be even solvent by May will
entail huge effort and larger luck. If I can't have car in NY for our winter
tour of sad Galloway I shall surely shed tears for first time since mothers
death in 1936. There are 27 seperate items I must attend before Jan.1, this
is but SF too. Booming south may prove necessary with loss of time and more
hassles. All this need I struggle to straighten and prevent inconvenience
of plans, there is yet hope all can be made well, actually it the whole thing
hinges on car and money. So, bah!
   Enfolded in bleak Obispo and blank Hinkle's household for the second
time in less than 2 months, 2weeks and 10 days respectively, I had nothing
to blast but Melville and Céline. In one sitting, (poor ass) of 30 hours I
took between my ears Moby Dick from end to end, while forcing into my belly-
where it settled so sour--the inanely sick diologue of Helen and Al. This
copy of Herman's Hankering was a magnificent Modern Library giant with great
pen-and-ink illustrations. Of course, I was inclinaed not to enthuse over
the old boy too much and certainly picked him up offhandily for I'd read it
all long ago. Then too, the new school hangup (remember a certain lecture
we attended on MD) and all the hustlebustle of his recent rediscovery made
me pretty sure I wouldn't find another mystery to delve, and I didn't. I
simply had a nice ordinary period of reading except that as I read I replaced
certain words, admired others, and all in all went thru the thing as one
author digging another for help, yet critically. One new impression,
especially when compared to long-ago reading; he is simple, writes so simple
and is very simple to understand. Its wonderful that he is so, would that I
was as clear, would too that I had his strength as I have his philosophy
and death knowledge. Céline too, I knew again, hasn't got it like good ole
Tommy boy, yet Ferdy is purty and his humor's a zoomer. Naturally, there is
nothing I can tell you about this trio(long tom, big tom, lunging plunging
gaping gulping grasping gone gurgleboy tom, but best; Tasty Tommy. Dirty
Ferdy, filthy ferdy, lousy louie, looney louie, lecherous louie, lazy louie,
lucky louie, blue Lou, limpin' lou, ad infinitum or ad nauseum or et al or
etc or on and on and so forth about C. Huge herman, humpback herman, hardy
herman, hasty herman, hamstrung herman, healthy herman, hallalulah herman,
Spermy Herman, Mammy Herman, holy herman,--dammit, I saved the best
nickname for Melville until last, and in fact got the idea for this whole
parentheses from it, now what? I just forgot it completely that all, fapdratit
. --thats a period, whazza matter, you can't see or sumpin?(flip for flappy

Less than 5 years ago I met my true love. The winter of 1945 had already buffeted Denver for a considerable time when this momentous event occured. Still retaining the shreds of the imposing position held some years before by unceasing philosophating, I was engaged in streching the rags of my regal robes over the remnents of old pupils. This I did to exist. Those young hoodlums to whom I'd once been master had turned to other things, and it was a hard task to convert their weakened concern into crumbs of refuge Now the juice of preachery was withered into dry appeals for generosity. The weather forced mornings in the library, afternoons in the poolroom, evenings at the bar. Copious with ~~loads~~ and hunger I would leave the readingroom's quietude and hurry three short blocks to the poolhall. Here I lolled on the hard onlooker's bench, waiting for a mark. When an approachable one did show, and I succeeded, I would prolong the meal he bought me. Otherwise, and also, I subsisted on theived candy bars and an occasional free pop. Come evetide I attached myself to the first available group touring the taverns--preferably in a car. It so happened that the week or so prior to meeting my oneheart I was sleeping in the begrudged sanctuary of a former student's automobile. On the morning of The Day I awoke in a particularly frigid state cramped upon the backseat of the unheated car. This, and the stress of previous months of such existence, almost made me decide to take off my hair shirt for awhile. Lying there, I contemplated for a bit the possibilities so doing. Then this image on my mind's surface led me to recall that the day held a major event. It was a semi-permanent setup I had with my younger Bloodbrother, an almost weekly change of clothes. I quickly unhinged myself and made for his home. Winter stillness froze my ears and sharp rareified air burned my throat as I pounded the pathway of the skeletonized public park bordering the benifactor's. Entering the house in the usual fashion via a third storey attic window I had to again prove my unusual skill at climbing. As a boy in eastside Denver I bettered every tree that I saw was worth conquering, save one old giant which resisted my efforts for years, until one fine night when I was well past the tree-climbing age---but, that is another tale to be told at another time. Kneeling in the garret's dust and restraining my quickened breath as best I could to prevent detection by the jazzy jealous woman he called mother, or the bull-necked liqour salesman stepfather, I rapped a soft signal over my clothes-agent's bedroom. He came up shorly and soon I was inside the too-big trousers and supplementary equipment he'd brought. Once again he marvelled in undertones that I'd acheived my difficult route made now impossible, he reasoned, by the wet snow clinging to my narrow clutchholds. Pleased, I departed with care to avoid excessive stain to my borrowed finery. The toll of my improvised ladder was not too high and I found but a few small damp spots after dropping to the ground from the last of the useable building ornaments.

Now, on the preceeding evening I had been occupying the rumble seat of a friend's roadster as he eased along downtown steets, in second gear, looking for a pickup. Driving slowly around the corner of 15th and Tremont sts., we spied a likely blonde swishing across the intersection. Robert Parlez parle to the lovely and she bounced in at once. Off we flew to the outskirts and a particular field just beyond the city limits. I got the broad's phone number and then played the stranger so if Bob's hasty, and usually undenied, assault failed I wouldn't be too fouledup when I called her later. Well, he more or less made out and we all drove back to town in half-amiable spirits. Before we dropped her at a hotel in the 1300 block on Broadway she had laid down a sloppy story about losing her purse and being completely broke. Bob wouldn't part with a sous and I had none so it did her no good to babble on. I decided then to fall by her hotel room the next day if there was nothing better to do at that time.

And I did. After leaving the clothes-hound I started for Broadway. Nearing the hotel I realized I was almost beside the Emily Griffith Opportunity school where a certain friend I had made while attending classes last year was about to break from a class. I thought it better to bypass Broadway for the moment and lounge in front of the school on the chance I might see him and get some coffee. I rounded the corner and saw my friend at once. He was leaning into the window of a 1940 Chevrolet sedan parked at the curb.

(3)

I was introduced to the soldier behind the wheel who was the car's lone occupant. His name was Kenneth Collins, a stocky tough looking little guy who had knew my friend for years. He was on a 10-day pass and looking for women. I told him I was on my way to a girl's room and said he could come along and take over if he wanted to. He liked the idea and we drove to her place, went up the stairs, and knocked on her door. At first she told me to go away and refused to open, but I talked for a few minutes and she gave in.

I walked into the room and saw a vision. Aperfect beauty of such love-liness that I forgot everything else and immediately swore to forgo all my ordinary pursuits until I made her. Desire instensely burned from my stunned eyes when I met her first glance from those light brown cowpools. Then I knew who she was, Jennifer Jones, only much more voluptuous with full tits and rounded ass. Amazing! a perfect real reproduction of Jennifer Jones on the edge of the bed. Oh Jack, everything went along so nicely, as I think of it I just bubble. What I mean is the other babe, whom I'd met the night before, and Kenny hit it off great right from the start and this left me free to devote my whole mind to Jennifer. In fact so powerfully did I make myself felt that all four of us soon knew there was to be little bullshit between us and instinctively we all tried to cure our souls by a pure affair. JJones name was Joan Anderson, she came from a small midwestern town some weeks before on the first trip she'd ever made. She was approaching 20 and very innocent. The virginity of her entire nature shone thru to me as clearly as a virtue, altho I saw she was nearly 5 months in pregnancy.

Within an hour this incredibly shy creature was bashfully installed beside me in the booth of a jumping joint. While Kenny and his box danced, Joan unlimbered to my massage and as she floated on her gentle comedown I was bursting to blow. We soon left the bar and slipped into K.'s snug Hotel where the at once retired retired to bed with bottle. I was commiss-ioned to take K's car back to his brothers and Joan accompanied me. My excitement as I drove penetrated Joan's bellyand she began to approach the peak I was on. The long return walk contained all the combination of illusions that makes young blood so prone to boil. One of those rare periods of sensation everyone has felt, the air, the girl, the hope. She put me straight on her condition; usual stuff, hi-school boy she'd known for years, first time, left home because it started to show, etc. Sad and weeping for so long, her eyes had disremembered sparkle. The talk sure knowledge, vowed of our eternal union made but sparks of splintered joy come out her suffered flintholes.

Back at the hotel we walked into a bounding bed on which K and his partner were going at it in a big way. They didn't pause for greeting or in anyway acknowledge our presence, just kept ripping away at 80 per. I was twitching with eagerness as Joan and I snuck into the offside of the double bed. I didn't rush, didn't push, (much) didn't force and only held her in firm tender caress. With one hand gently clasping her bottom and the other supporting her back I kissed the sweet face and lips then pro-gressed my mouth to the heavy breasts, while my enormous cock slid under the silk slip and pounded against the soft belly pressed under me. She was still so young the couple beside us bothered her, so I did not fuck then, but kept at what I was doing for an hour or so. Finally K and his left us to go eat and we wasalone, yet I wisely contained myself from all-out attack for we had been tense for so long and the edge of thrill worn off just enough so that to do it now would not please her perfectly. I pointed this out and she agreed later that night would indeed be wonderfully right.

K and girlie came back and we all went jumping on his money. Joan and I were in fine accord and her eyes were now shining full with joyous love. We planned and planned, there was no limit all we had to do was begin. The next morning, after a night of licking the platter clean, K decided he'd had enough of his lovely and abruptly kicked her out. I could have stayed on with him for the few days before he went back to camp and I sadly needed a roof for each transient night, but Joan must stay with her friend until she was settled and, not to leave my mate, I followed the girls onto the icy streets.

(4)

Neither of them knew a connection for some loot and mine had been pushed to the limit where they would have guffawed loudly at my asking for an actual cash dollar, especially for a silly waste like a hotel room. We walked for some time, then, offhand, Joan mentioned a cab driver who'd tried to father her some weeks before. She recalled his name and I got her right on the ball. Making contact by cab-phone she arranged to meet him at 4 o'clock when he got off duty. We passed the time until then (3 or 4 hours) in Kenny's hotel lobby, and when Joan left to make the meet, her buddy and I stayed there to be out of the cold. Our most optomistic wishes were more than confirmed as my beauty returned in good time with money in her purse and supper in her mixer. The old boy (about 50) was really fatherly alright, happily married and with an amount of dough, he just gushed with pity at my poor innocent's plight and his wallet was touched too. Knowing I could sneak in and out at any hour in my old haunt, (one of many such) the Denver hotel, I told the girls to rent the cheapest weekly room there. Then began the tragedy.

Purposely I have not said much about Joan's girlfriend, the one I'd met first you understand. Altho she wouldn't give out with it on the intial night, the next day her high nasel twang proclaimed the name of Mary Lou Berle. I had spent the winter of 1942 in the Ozarks and knew her hometown of Big Springs, Mo.and without another ear to bend that was familiar with that section of country her homesick mind really poured the blurb to me. Acouple of years before, at 16, she'd left home and hitchiked to Springfield Mo. and got a job on the local radio station singing those horrible hill-billy songs every 6 A.M. This didn't last too long and she'd tramped here and there in the midwest until she met Joan and together they had Greyhound to Denver. Let me tell you, boy, I know there is nothing like a fine old mountain ballad, but when Mary Lou got drunk (nightly) and began "The Maple on the Hill" in yodeling screech,as her frosty blue eyes wept buckets, my cringing belly would curl into a genuine Gordion Knot. Not that she wasn't a lovely; blonde hair well bleached, smooth facial features, altho pancake madapskin was much too dry, 5' 2" figure, but the too-small breasts were more than compensated by the oversize ass so her weight, I judge, while just outside 123 3/4 lbs. did not yet, I suspect, approach 126 lbs., unless, of course, my hasty estimate is inaccurate,then, naturally, I allow you, nay, urge, that you draw your own conclusions about her avoirm du pois. Amen, and may god rest ye merry gentlemen. Speaking of Miss Berle's behind I must say here that the one quality of it, indeed, the sole property by which I remember her whole body, was an exquisite overfleshiness that is not too often found. The tempting jelly of her physical self paralleled her entire spiritual being in that the excessive soft mass made for too much matter thru which to wade, and this adequate defense defeated my most wonderfully casual attack; since I was not a perfect fool. We became buddies with our guard up.

Installed in the Denver hotel Joan and I continued our bliss for the first few days. We planned a highway walk soon to Ft. Collins where I was to drive truck and she would work at some little available thing. Able to move in my hat,I had quickly gotten my gear together, Joan washed her few clothes, packed them in her one suitcase and we decided we were ready. Nonetheless, since we still had 3 or 4 days of free rent left, we continued in much the same routine. Joan was quietly content to stay in the hotel room most of the time, she sewed baby clothes and read a bit from the books I had. Mary Lou was quite another way, early in the day she left and made the bars looking for men. I followed my usual habits, poolhall; occasional chiseled meal, drink, carride, show, snooker game. Going about this business I began a depression which sharply constrasted with the Joan idyl. This, intrinsicly, was to be expected,only perhaps not so soon. I knew, intuitively, I was not the one for her, not now anyhow. She was too good for me of course, but all that sort of thing means nothing, and besides, depends on the way one looks at it. My particular viewpoint opposed the warp in both of us, the shame was, being young and hard, I could become unmitigatingly brutal while morbidly suffering my love's pathos.   the

Quickly it happened, and so powerfully that after I broke,opening dike there seemed no way to plug the gap and I was helplessly embroiled and carried away by the plunging torrent from a bursted dam.

(3)

Seldom have I experienced more emotion and never have I witnessed a girl's
heart broken so completely. HA

I had returned from the poolhall about 7 PM. Entering the girls' 11th
floor room(top floors of hotels are always best) I found Joan, Mary Lou
and a tough young sailor sailor she had picked up. Mary L. was half-drunk,
the navyman slightly, and Joan not at all. (as I recall J. neither smoked
nor drank, being a lady she didn't cuss either) I called my love aside and
out of the blue told her I'd been thinking it over and maybe it would be
better if she went to Fort Collins alone when the rent came due tomorrow.
Straight off her complexion changed, pale lips quivered, then grimaced as
tears sprung. From out incredulous eyes came stricken disbelief. I decided
to take a bath. I had barely gotten in the hot tub when Mary Lou stormed
along the short hallway and pounded on the bathroom door, yelling to be
let in at once. I opened to her and without preamble she tore into me at a
furious rate. "Joan just told me you were leaving her and she's sittin' in
there crying fit to die. You son-of-a-bitch, I knew you had a dirty look in
your eye when you called her out in the hall. You goddam bastard,get up out
of that tub and go in there and tell her you didn't mean it, you lousy cock-
sucking prick, or else I'll beat the shit out of you,and if I can't do it I'll
get my boyfriend in there to help me and we'll pound your face in together,
you motherfuckin' cheapskate" She went on and on, getting hotter every minute
and coming up with a really fine collection of words, a string of names for
me poured from her angry red mouth that still tingle the brain. At first I
tried to reason with her, then I got a little mad and asked her by what manner
of presumption did a stupid whore like herself justify preaching to me, especially in such bitchy threats? This almost did me in good; I saw at once
I'd make a mistake. She bellowed out, "right? threat? Why you stinking bum,
I see the way your treating that fine girl and you expect me to just stand
there? It doesn't matter what I am, you chickenshit little yellowbellied
bastard, but, by god, I'll show you who I am!" And with this she pounced
on me. Standing in the slippery tub, I had difficulty holding her off right
away and she got in a couple of good licks before I could halt her onslaught.
As she scratched my nude body while struggling to get her hands free from my
grip, I kept worrying that she would take it in her head to give me the knee.
She didn't, just shoved her feet face up to mine and spluttered,"threats?"
over and over. I had her under control soon enough, but daren't let go; at
one point she did manage to break away for a moment by biting my shoulder and
then suddenly lowering her head to deliver a strong butt to my midriff. I
"ooffed", but caught her again before she could get the door unlocked.
Finally she tired and I said I'd let her go if she promised to be quiet and
sit down and talk sensibly. The little spitfire agreed and sank to the stool
(not the toilet, you silly ass Mr. Kerouac, but a simple small wooden three
legged stool, 13 inches high; milkmaids made them famous in the 18th century
and many cheap hotels place them in their bathrooms to have the guests put
all their clothes and bath paraphenalia in a proper heap;accomodations!) with
exhausted murder burning from her distainful eyes. Well, you can wager your
ass I talked fast. I cloud(that's a quaint misspelling) could could could
see my itzy-bitzy lovespat might begin to assume monsterous porportions,
not only would M.L. and her sailorboy be happy to give me a workingover, but
it could even happen that I'd be kicked out in the cold Denver night. Foolish
boy that I was, these were the simple fears in my mind as I dressed and
returned to the room with Mary Lou to put out the fire. Little did I guess
that the night was to gallop from this small flareup onward untill at the
darkest hour we would all be engulfed in hellfire and when dim dawn first
declared itself, singed (I say, bud, that's singe with a d, you understand)
to doom, I was to be scourged by nightmares of my clinker soul.

Joan seemed too easy to placate, I was suspicious and tho nothing but
romance had passed between us before, thus giving me no previous ground upon
which to base a judgement of her natural reaction to harshness, my rebuttal
had hurt her too much for the present calm to be genuine. Before I began
blurting a mealy-mouthed apology, before, in fact, I had hardly opened my
blubberblabbers she stopped me with,"its alright, honey, I've forgotten everything allready." I did, however, mumble through nice cozy job of "forgive me".
The whole thing was too easy, as I said, and being leery of her quietude I
felt further explosions beneath her outward composure.

(8)

I only wished, a vain punk, that she would content herself with a martyr
attitude so that I might be spared the bickering of an emotional young girl.
ad I not avoided her pain-filled eyes perhaps I would not have been guilty
of such a gross underestimation of this woman's character.

Joan urged me go go back and finish my bath and I did. While washing
I realized even more fully how I'd put my foot in it and dreaded to face
her when I returned to the room. But she came to face me, that is, as I was
dressing after the bath she knocked on the door. Her haggard features were
in strained repose as she entered and I saw she was about to breakdown again.
She began quietly enough, asking what I was going to do now and if I'd come
to Fort Collins and see her sometime. I protested that I'd go there with her,
or whatever she wanted, but it was no good, she read the lie in my eye.
Slowly she wept, deeply she wept, long lashes could not contain the eyes
lament. Even were I nice enough to stay with her, she told me, she knew why
I didn't love her. I was too good for her and she wasn't good enough for me.
(all right now, you sloppy critic Jack, stop reading. That last sentence,
to put you in the know and set the matter straightso you can intelligently
point your finger at it and giggle like a silly french fool--you better have
orgasms reading this, or bawl like a baby--is the crux of the whole thing.
Yessir, she thought I was toogood for her and believed it so strongly that
all the subsequent happening follow from this single idea. Rememberance of
my Joan's thinking she wasn't good enough for me, so stupidly juvinile,hope-
lessly romantic, intellectually blind and such a preposterous untruth that
I'm convinced it will save her soul, is the reason I chose to write you this)

I was stunned, even shocked! I knew she must be joshing, but I saw no
joke in her eye. "What?", I said, "your kidding, you don't know what your
saying, I'm a full bastard not a half-breed. Where is your eyes? your mind?
can't you guess what a filthy rat I am? Don't be silly, look at yourself,
youre wonderful, perfect and so good it amounts to dumbness. Stop this hogwash, sheer nonsense, why, a hundred of you couldn't hold a candle to my evil!
You get the idea, Jackieboy, I put it on thick because I was really surprised.
It all did no good, she clung with stubborn perversity to the "no good" theme
in one form or the other. Becoming more deadly serious,as more than an hour
steamed by in that overheated bath, her intensity at last gave me the clue
for which I had been groping since she'd first uttered that emotionbacked
statement. I'd obviously disregarded all preceeding hints by her embarrassed
and retiring manner as simply the ordinary guilt suffered by an introverted
girl experiencing her first wrong. One could clearly see the effects of her
pregnancy had made her again a frightened lonely little girl who fairly melted
with shame. Noindeedjx, there was no doubt as to the true nature of her flaw,
a schoolboy would even sense it, and altho I'd known she felt guilty above
all else, I hadn't much bothered about it. After all, one sees young ladies
(not used advisedly; the word ladies I mean, you drunken Theaded ignoramus.)
like that daily and it is the accepted--demanded, by golly,--normal way for
them to feel and act when in Joan's position. (everyone applaud Dr. Cassady.)
It was just that I hadn't guessed the enormity of her guilt-feeling. The
immensity of it struck home with all its glory. Suddenly, as I sat there,
(me on the stool and her perched on the toilet cover;got that this time?)
listening to this beautiful young female tear her sweet heart to ribbons
because her gentle mind could not cope with the overwhelming fear that
disgrace had brought to her, I knew she was lost. All had come about when
a sallow kid's cock dribbled 2 seconds of sperm, which she hadn't enjoyed,
into her spicy nest--the fragrance of which I was smelling at that moment.
As she droned on, almost oblivious to me now, I stared into her soul. My
Joan would never know peace again, the germ of the present unsurmountable
preoccupation with self-debasement planted in her by unwitting parents had
blossomed into the bloom that splits the mind. I bemoaned the loss of this
child.

Abruptly Joan said, "I love you, Neal, goodbye," and dashed out the bathrm
I stayed in my stooled position, cramped with a vision of unecessary waste.
Absorbed in vacantheaded digestion of the sad sickness in her mind, I failed,
at first, to hear the scream. Then I heard two anguished wails,"Neal,Neal."
I jumped up and opened the door with real terror encased in my bowels. It
was Mary Lou, tears gushing down her cherry chipmunk cheeks smeared her horr-

(7)

bly thick face powder. I saw the ghastly stain of death shoot out from stricken
sockets, puffed lids enclosed beady eyes of accusation. "What have you done to her?
Why did you do it? What did you say, what did you say?" She raved on, standing there in the hall, her unbelivably blownup face now bent into the quivering
palms of dirtblack hands. She was all in a lump and slobbering in hysterical
panic. I shook her, "what happened, what happened?" I could hardly believe
this silly cunt would become so scared just because, as I suspected, Joan had
gathered her things and left. For a minute or two I able to get no coherancy
from her, she threw herself on the filthy floor carpet all in pieces. As I
dropped her and started for the room she rose up to screech, "She's dead, she's
dead, and you killed her," then fell back to her sobbing.
    I didn't hurry, there seemed no need to. Walking the short corridor my
thought was, "why aren't there any people? With all this noise there should
be heads out every door making a hellofa racket thenselves just finding out
what the fuss is about". So Joan has killed herself; I opened the door calmly.
There was the sailor, leaning out the window, breathing hard. No words were
spoken, I started toward him and then saw he had Joan's feet in his hands.
I hurried to help and together we pulled her back into the room, her dress
was over her head and I looked at her damp crotch, so dark and tempting, as
I tugged on her delicious legs. The sailor stared too, but was somewhat
embarrassed I do believe. We laid her on the bed and smoothed her garments.
Green foam was on her lips, her eyes were closed, she was lying motionless.
Now, as I told you earlier, Mr. JLK, the blonde Mary Lou was that way only
by regular dousing with bleach. The sailor (no name) said that my raven-
haired Joan, really most deeply black, had come into the room and evidenced
an interest in MLB's bleach bottles, reading the labels, asking if they were
indeed posionous, etc. There was two bottles, one, hydrogen peroxide, and the
other, spirits of Ammonia. They, naturally, were one of danger,
and altho she gulped of both bottles, she drank mostly of the Ammonia.
Gasping from the effects of her stark cocktail, and already vomiting out her
stomach's contents, she pretended to let the sailor and Mary Lou help her.
As soon as Joan was seated Mary Lou had rushed out to announce her death.
Taking advantage of this momentary diverting of the sailor's attention, Joan
had jumped up and scrambled for the window determined to throw herself out.
Needless to say the sailor siezed her number seven's, lucky size, as
they were disappearing from view and managed to hold on until I arrived.
By the narrowest of margins he had saved her, by the merest of coincidences
he was in the room at all, and now by the slightest of signs I watched her
return to life. She stirred, moaned, and was soon puking again, all over
the bed, herself and the floor. We were easing her retching as best we could
when the door opened and in walked swollen Mary and two big men. They were
the night manager and his assistant, whom M.Lou had summoned, she had finished
mopping the hall floor with herself. To my surprise neither of them were
gruff or threatening at all, instead they tried to soothe everything over as
if it was their fault Joan had attempted suicide. The room was a mess, everything topsy-turvy, and these big lummoxes must not have known there were hotel
maids each morning for they began hustling about, picking up things and cleaning in a frenzy. The sailor and I pitched in to help them, as Mary patted
Joan's sunken countenance. Bustling around straightening rumpled rugs, righting overturned chairs, emptying ashtrays and the like, I kept thinking how
strange this was. Surely I could be doing something more productive than
wasting time stumbling about a room that would be taken care of in a few hours
anyhow by women hired for just such a purpose. I began to work up a little
fantasy that I shouldn't be doing this; what would the union say, putting a
poor nigger out of a job. I must emphasize how really friendly these hotel
men were; even if we didn't have any money we could stay on after tomorrow if
Joan was too sick to move, they would call a doctor if we liked, told us not
to worry about the disturbance we'd made, etc. They didn't quiz the sailor
and myself being in the girls room at midnight, didn't mention suicide and
acted as tho Joan had just fallen ill from something she ate, and, in fact,
soon left us to our own devices as they bowed and smiled out the door.
    Some time before the December events I'm reciting--in the late spring
of 1944, May and June to be exact--I drove a truck delivering laundry supplies
My employers, the Carmen distributing Co., had large barrels of Ammonia.

(8)

One of these I spilled while handling one day. I'm sure you've smelled liquid spirits of A., but perhaps not had your nostrils exposed to a large amount of it all at once. The considerable quantity of ammonia that gurgled out of the barrel, even tho I wiped up most of it, make me sick as hell as zI worked over the puddle all day. Being so conditioned, when I entered Joan's follyroom I found it honest torture to endure its potent aroma. Don't think I'm one to give out with a lot of bullshit about a smell, altho I wish, of course, that I could blow about one for 20 pages like Proust did. But I got to tell you that second only to the "no good" speech of Joan's, this ammonia kick is the closest to my rememberance. From the first whiff my head ached, my ears pounded, my eyes burned, my heart banged against a heaving chest. And it grew worse the longer I lingered in that accursed room.

Meantime, Joan was very sick; the weak angel muttered constantly and was not entirely concious. We debated getting her to a hospital, but didn't, we argued over giving her an antidote, but didn't; we discussed how badly ammonia posioning might affect one who had survived more than an hour and were optomistic that she had been regurgitating steadily. Never having heard of anyone dying from consuming "more than half a qt. bottle" (as Mary claimed) of spirits of A., I talked us all into a hopeful idea that she would just be sickashell for a while; placing much emphasis on the fine puke job Joan was doing. So happy did they become, except, of course, my stupored Joan, that the quiet sailor said he may as well go out and get another bottle of whiskey. All my body hated to leave the heated building at 2 AM, but I knew I'd combated that damn deathagent,SofA, long enough,(incidentally, the smell didn't seem to bother the other two much) and, besides, this was my best chance of breaking away from the hasslebeast, Mary Lou. I reasoned Joan wouldn't be good for anything the rest of the night and if I felt it was necessary I could always come back later to help her get treatmentat DGHosp. So, I told the sailor I'd accompany him on his errand, since I needed some ain He said OK, Mary Lou didn't seem to mind, and so I left my limp lover laid low.

Once outside, I let the sailor know I'd see him later, if he was still in the room that night, and took off on the morning streets. In the back of my mind I had been dickering with the idea of busting in on Kenny Collins sister. I couldn't bring myself to wake her at this hour until after I'd tramped the cold for quite a while. The poolhall and bars were closed, but I easily might have found some warm spot to lounge in, apt. houses, etc., if it hadn't been that I was holding out for a bed to flop on; especially with the outside hope of a girl in it. The trouble was I only knew her casually, I met her when, a few days before, Kenneth stopped by to feed both of us at the restaurant where she was a waitress. I knew her address, it was the same hotel Ken had stayed in; I even knew her room, number 313. There was no difficulty getting in the hotel and there was no night clerk. I found her door and knocked carefully, she opened without even asking who was there. Seeing she recognized me,(I had been afraid she wouldn't, since she wore very thick-lensed glasses) I started an exciting tale of drink and suicide to get her interested. Ending with big complaints about my horrible ammonia illness, having no money, etc., I asked to sleep on her floor. She was amiable enough, but to allay the fisheye I thought I glimpsed under her hairless brows, I gave quick promises to try no tricks in the dark. This must have pleased her and she said sure, only come on to bed,"because I have no blankets for the floor and I can take care of myself if you pull anything funny". Ordinarily I am not one to diddle away much time under these circumstances and I lay it to them right away, and this one was so easy too, but, better than miscue,I protected my interests by going to sleep. We got up about noon and I walked her to the cafe, and my interest paid off, she bought breakfast. We jawed a bit, then I sauntered to the poolhall.

When I checked in some of the boys asked what was new, I said nothing and held my peace. I'd buttoned my lip because I wanted to mull over the whole last 24 hours. This sort of thing was habit, I often spent entire PM's sitting there, and while watching the finesse of the billiard players, the dash of the pool players bashing into their game and the cautious click of the red balls the snooker players favored, mused. All the games going at once nagged for my attentionso that my distracted brain had developed the practice of escaping into the oblivion of ponder. Faroff wonderings at life to

(9)

contrast with nearby obvious enchantment at display of skill. Vague fancies
gave complicated angle-shots off my skull, as plain spheres get questick
banked off the green-clothed hard rubber. I decided to return to the D.hotel.

On the way up to the room the night manager stopped me to say my friends
had left that noon. They were gone. I questioned him; Joan had been hauled
away in an ambulance about 10 AM, he didn't know who called it or from what
hospital it was, and Mary Lou had departed shortly after. The sailor wasn't
mentioned. I thanked him and went back to the poolhall, it was now about 7 PM
and I had to start conning a place to sleep. There were no prospects, so I
left to get to KCollins sister by 10, the time she got off work. I spent
that, and several succeeding, nights with her and didn't goofoff this time,
but went right to it. Altho she was a pure Okie, her charms were very real
and we got along OK. There was no fumbling, she feed me when I walked her
to work each 2PM and again when I met her at KX 10; between these hours I
haunted the poolhall.

One freezing afternoon, about a week after my new routine had begun,
a taxicab doubleparked and its short driver pushed into the place. I saw
this uniformed midget talk with the proprieter then walk straight for me.
He asked if I was Cassady and said he had a message for me, "Joan Anderson
is in room 9 at St. Luke's hospital and wants you to visit her". He turned
and left before I could thank him. Because I'd been lucky enough to get
inside the pants of a few St. Luke nurses(this before the Gullions,too) I
happened to know that hospital's visiting hours; so saved a nickel, or a walk.
I knew it was too late to go that day and decided to go the next, but hungup
in the poolhall the next day,I didn't go. Nor did I make it the following
afternoon; I kept hoping for a buddie with a car to be available about 2:30
when I showed at the PH, and there was never one there before visiting hours
were over--about 3:30 or 4, I forget now. The walk was only about a half
mile, but I keep thinking maybe a car would turn up in a day or two so I
could avoid the cold. Well, a car never came and I was reduced to saying to
myself, "I'll go tomorrow anyhow". But I never did, until---

Goddammybloodysoul, Jack, I just this very second remember something.
Every incident in this pricky tearjerker(for the hero who is demmed because
he's such an awful bastard) is exactly true as I'm writing it; except one
thing: What I now recalltoo late to rewrite is that when I want back to
the Denver hotel that next afternoon the three of them were still in the
room all right, but a few minutes after I got there Joan was taken to St.
Lukes in an ambulance and the man who'd arranged it and paid the billxer for
everything was that fatherly cabdriver, the midget I speak of above. He
drove M.Lou and myself to the hospital in his taxi, following the ambulance.
We waited an hour or so while Joan was being admitted -I never saw her, save
for those few minutes in the Hroom-- then, we all left and he dropped us
downtown. The point is I knew where she was all the time I was going thru
the above poolhall paragraph. Now go on with this nonsense, if I've got
the strengh to, you must; after all, you're the poor sucker who asked for it.
(here comes the part where Joan's cabby comes to the poolhall to get me,
the message was, "get your ass up there and see that sick girl, she's crying
for you and if you don't get off your lazy butt and go yourself I'll be in
here in a day or two and drag you there myself".) --So I went to see her.
TO MAKE THIS SOMEWHAT CLEARER: only one message--the latter--and PH, 23 lines
above, means poolhall. Please figure it out if you can, buddy, I'm going on.

To have seen a spectre isn't everything, one does it semi-annually,
and there are deathmasks piled,one atop the other, clear to heaven. Commoner
still are the wan visages of those returning from the shadow of the valley
This means little to those who have not lifted the ninth veil. The ward
nurse cautioned me not to excite her(how can one prevent that?) and I was
allowed only a few minutes. The headnurse also stopped me to say I was per-
mited to see her just because she always called my name and I must cheer her.
She had had a very near brush and was not rallying properly, actually was
in marked decline,and still much in danger. Quite impressed to my duties,
I entered and gazed down on her slender form resting so quietly on the high
white bed. Her pale face was whiter; like chalk. It was extremely apparent
how utterly weak she was, there seemed absolutely no blood left in her body.

(10)

I stared and stared, she didn't breath, didn't move; I would never have recognized her, she was a waxen mummy. White is the absence of all color, she was white; all white, unless beneath the covers, whose top carressed her breasts, was hidden a speck of pink. The thin ivory arms which tapered inwarded until they reached the slight outward bulge of narrow palms, and the hands in turn bent inward with a more sharp taper only to quickly end in long fingers curled to a point. These things, and her head, with its completely matted hair so black and contrasting with all the whiteness, were the only parts of her visible. Quite normal, I know, but I just couldn't get over how awfully dead she looked. I had so arranged my head above hers that when her eyes opened, after about 10 minutes, they were in direct line with mine; they showed no surprise, nor changed their position in the slightest. The faintest of smiles, the merest of voices, "hello". I placed my hand on her arm, it was all I could to restrain myself from jumping up on the bed to hold her. I saw she was too weak to talk and told her not to, I, however, rambled on at a great rate. There was no doubt she was overjoyed to see her eyes said so. It was as though the gesture of self-destruction had, in her mind, equalized all the guilt. The courage of committing the act seemed to have justified her to herself. This action on her conviction, no matter how neurotic, had called for all her strength and she was now released. Free from the urge, since the will-for-death needs strong concentrate of pressure to fulfill itself, and once accomplished via attempt, was defeated until another period of buildup is gone thru; unless, of course, one succeeds in reaching death the first shot, or is really mad. Gazing down on her, with a grin of artificial buoyancy, I sensed this and felt an instant flood of envy. She had escaped, at least for some time, and I knew I had yet to make my move. Being a coward I had postponed too long and I realized I was further away from commitance than ever. Would hesitancy never end? She shifted her cramped hand, I looked down and for the first time noticed the tight sheet covered a flat belly. It was empty, sunken; she had lost her baby. For a moment I wondered if she knew it, then, thought she must know--even now she was almost touching her stomach, and she'd been in the hospital 10 days-- surely a stupid idea. I resolved to think better. (I've already prolonged this silly paragraph too long for no good reason and am displeased as hell in the way the writings coming out, so---) The nurse glided up and said I'd better go; promising to return next visiting day, I leaned over and kissed Joan's clear forehead and left. (I repeat, dammit all, I didn't say a single thing I wanted to; bunk! baaaa, grrrrr, horseshit.)

Off to the poolhall, back to the old grind; I seemed to have a mania. From the way I loafed there all day one would scarcely believe I'd never been in a poolhall 2 short years ago before; why, less than six months ago I still couldn't bear to play more than one game at a time. Well, what is one to say about things he has done? I never again went back to the hospital to bless Joan, oh, thats what I felt like; blessing her. Each day I lacerated myself thinking on her, but I didn't go back. "Sometimes I sits and thinks, other times I sits and drinks, but mostly I just sits". I must have been in a pretty bad way.

Anyhow, two more weeks went by in this fashion, my inability to stir from my poolhall prison became a joke, even to me. It was the night before christmas, about 5 PM, when a handsome woman near 40 came inside the gaol's (so it might be misspelled, so its old english and this is modern Denver, so its straight out of Wilde's "Ballard of Reading, Reding, Readding, Redding, gaol", or right from Dickens(Charlie my boy, chipper Charlie, cheerie Charles, Christian Charley, chuckles Chuck, Christmasie Dickensie, etc, etc, etc.) or a hundred others who used the word, so its pronounced "jail", so why not put jail, what a question, what a question, you illiterate immigrant, you blarsted bum--rum bum, that is, Bayrumbum,-you marvelously married man, any bloody fool can see jail doesn't start with a "g" and gaol does and besides showing off my learning is absolutlypositivlyunquestionably necessary for the next word that follows it in this gripping thriller, then too, I gotta save "jail" for use in its proper place on the next page, and I'll have to watchout overdoing it, I've already put down stir, prison and gaol, so leave it in; gaol, that is.) gates and asked for me.

(11)

I went up front to meet her, as I came closer I saw she was better than handsome, a real goodlooker despite her age. She introduced herself, said she was a friend of Jaon (now see, that goddam gaol, which I first wrote as goal--you can easily spy the erasure--has gotten my flappy(bottom of page 1) typing all floppy) JoanJoanJoanJoan Anderson and invited me to dinner. My heart bounced with guilty joy, I accepted and we walked the 5 blocks to this fine though forty ladies' apt. at 1627 Lincoln St.. The fatherly taxidriver opened the door, my hostess siad (there I go again) said it was her husband and that Joan (careful, easy does it) would be out in a minute. Preparations for a huge dinner was in the making, I sat on the sofa and waited. The bathroom--ugly word--door swung out and before my eyes was once again the gorgeus "second" of Jennifer J. Fresh from the shower, mirror-primped, stepped my heroine resplendent in her new friend's housecoat. Just when you think you've learned your lesson and swear to watch your step, a single moment offguard will pop up and hope springs high as ever. One startled look and I knew I was right back where I started; I felt again that choking surge flooding me as when first I'd seen her. I started talking to myself, determined to whip the poolhall rut and drag my stinking ass out the hole.

Over the prosperous supper on which we soon pounced hung an air of excitement. Joan and I were leaping with lovelooks across the roastbeef, while cabby and wife beamed on us. And we planned, yessir, all four of us and right out loud too. I was kinda embarrassed at first when the host began without preamble,"Alright, you kids have wasted enough time, I see you love each other and you're going to settle down right now. In the morning Joan is starting at St. Lukes as a student nurse, she's told me thats what she would like to do. As for you, Neal, if you're serious, I'll get up a little early tomorrow and before I go to work we'll see if my boss will give you a job. If you can't get away with telling them you're 21--the law says you gotta be 21, you're not that old yet are you?,(I said no) so that you can drive taxi, you can probably get a job servicing the cabs. That OK with you?" I said certainly it was and thanked him; and everybody laughed and was happy.

It was further decided that Joan and I stay with theme until we got our first paycheck, we would sleep on the couch that opened out into a bed. Gorged with the big meal, I retired to the bathroom as the women did the dishes and the old man read the paper. (by golly, Jack, it seems everything I write about happens in a bathroom, don't think I'm hungup that way, its just the incidents exactly as they occured, and here is another one, because---) A knock on the toilet door and I rose to let in my resurrected beauty. She was as coy as ever, but removed were fear and embarrassment. We did a bit of smooching, then seated on the edge of the tub she asked if I wanted to see her scar. I kneeled before her to observe betteras she parted the bathrobe to reveal an ugly red wound, livid against her buttermilk belly, streching from the navel to clitorm She was worried I wouldn't think her as beautiful, or love her as much, now that her body had been marred by the surgeons knife performing a Ceasarian. There might have been a partial Historectomy too and she fretted that the production of more babies--"when we get the money"--would prove difficult. I reassured her on all counts, swore my love (and meant it) and finally we returned to the livingroom.

Oh, unhappy mind; trickster! O fatal practicality! I was wearing really filthy clothes, but had a change promised me by a friend who lived at 12th and Ogden Sts. So as not to hangup my dwarf savior when we went to see his buddyboss next AM, my foolish head thought to make a speedrun and get the necessary clean impediments now. Acting on this obvious need--if I was to impress my hoped-for employer into hiring me--I promised to hurry back, and left. Where is wisdom? Joan offered to walk with me, and I turned down the suggestion reasoning it was very cold and I could make better time alone, besides, she was still pretty weak, and if she was to work tomorrow the strain of the fairly long walk might prove too much,--no sense jepardizing her health. Would that I'd made her walk with me, would that she'd collapsed rather than let me go alone, would anything instead of what happened! Not only did the new promise for happiness go down the drain, and I lose Joan forever, but her peace was to evaporate once and for all, and she herself was to sink into the iniquity reserved for a certain type of beaten women.

(12)

I rushed my trip to the clothes-depot, made good connections and was
quickly on my way back to the warm apt., and my Joan. As you well know,Jack,
the route from 12th and Ogden to 16th and Loncolnsts.lies for the most part,
if one so desires, along E.Colfax Ave. Horrible mistake, stupid moment; I
chose that path just to dig people on the crowded thruugh thoroughfare as I
hustled by them. At midblock between Penna. and Pearl Sts. is a tavern whose
plateglass front ill-conceals the patrons of its booths. I was almost past
this bar when I glanced up to see my younger B.Brother inside drinking beer
alone. I had made good time and the hard habit of lushing that I was so
addicted to pushed me thru the door to bum a quickie off him. Surprise,
surprise, he was loaded with loot and, more surprising, gushed all over me.
He ordered as fast as I could drink, and I didn't let the waitmress stop,
finishing the glass in a gulp; one draught for the first few, then two for
the next sweral and so on until I was sipping normally by the time an hour
had fled. First off he wanted a phone number--the reason for his genorosity,
I suspect--and I was the only one who comld give it to him. He claimed to
have been sitting there actually brooding over the very girl on the other end
of this phone number, and I believed him; had to take it true, because for
the last five months it had become increasingly clear that he was hotashell
for this chick--who was my girl. I gave him the number and he dashed from
one booth to the other.(got that, old man, beerbooth to phonebooth) I had
cautioned him not to mention my name, nor tell her I was there, and he said
he wouldn't. But he did, altho he denied it laterx. mmm The reason for his
disloyalty, despite it cost me Joan, was justifiable since, as one will when
about to be denied a date of importance while drinking, he had used my whereabouts as a lastditch lure to tempt her out. He came back to the booth from
the booth (see here, phone booth to barbooth, don't you know--barbooth is a
terrific dicegame for highstaked illegal gambling in N.Denver, too, so there.)
crestfallen, she had said she couldn't leave the house just now, but to call
her back in a half-hour or so; this didn't cheer him as it would have me,
he's richer and less easily satismfied. He called her again, about 45 minutes
after I had first been pulled into the dive by my powerful thirst, and she
saidfor him to wait at this joint and she'd be down within an hour. This im
lenghof time didn't seem unreasonable, she lived quiteaways further out in
eastdenver. I thought everything was going perfectly. Bill got the girl, I
got my drinks and still had a short period of grace in which to slop up more
eforshe showed(I certainly didn't intend to be there when she arrived) and I'd
only be a little late returning to Joan where I'd plead hassel in getting
the clothes. Oh sad shock, oh unpleasant time; had I just not guzzled that
last beer all the following would not be written and I could end this story with,
"And they lived happily ever after".
     Whoa, old buddy, read slowly for a bit and have patiencewith my verbosity.
(if you haven't been slowed to a stop already by my stilted style, and too,
I mean more patience beyond that which you've needed for my unfunny parenthese
There are two things I've got to say here, one is a sidepoint and it'll come
second, the first is essential to the understanding of this unending trash;
so, I gotta bore you with one of my hollywood flashbacks--duller, in fact.
I'll leave out the most of it and be as brief as possible to make it tight,
altho, by the nature of it, this'll be hard--especially since I'm tired.
Number 1: On June 2, 1945 I was released fromm Colorado State Reformatory,
after doing 11 months and 10 days (know the song?) of hard labor. Soon after
returning to Denver I had the rare luck to meet a 16-year-old East hi beauty
who had well-to-do parents; a mother and pretty older sister to be exact.
Cherry Mary (Mary Ann Freeland) was her name because she lived on Cherry St.
and was a cherry when I met her. That condition didn't last long I ripped
into her like a maniac and she loved it. A tremendous affair, countless
countless things to be said about it--I can hardly help from blurting out
20 or 30 statements right now despite resolution to condense. I'm firm (ha)
and the story of our 5 months intercourse--with its many incidents that are
perculating this moment in my brain; about carnival-night we met (Elitch's),
the hundreds of mountain trips in her new mercury, rented trucks with mattress
in back, at her cabin, cabins I broke into, day I got her to bang Hal Chase,
time I gave her clap after momentous meeting between her and mother of my
second child(only boy before Diana's) time I knocked her up;and knocked it,

(13)

mad nights and early AM's at Goodyear factory I worked alone in from 4 PM
to anytime I wanted to go home, doing it on golfcourses, roofs, parks, cemetarys
(mispelled;you know, dead people's home) snowbanks, schools and schoolyards,
hotel bathrooms, her mother's vacant houses (she was realtor), doing it every-
way we could think of any-old-place we happened to be, in fact, we did it in
so many places that Denver was covered with our peckertracks; so many different
ones that I can't possibly remember, often we'd trek clear from one side of
town to another just to find a spot to drop to it, oh ordinary occasions,
however, I'd just pull it out and shove--to her bottom if we were secluded,
to her mouth if not, the greatest most humorous incident of the lot; to please
her mother she'd often babysit for some of their socially prominent and
wealthy friends several times a week, I drive out to that particular evening's
assignment, after she called to give the address and say the coast was clear,
(funny english joke; man and woman wife in livingroom, phone rings, man
answers and says he wouldn't know, better call the coast guard, and hangs up.
wife says, "who was it, dear?" and mans says, "I don't know, some damn fool
who wanted to know if the coast was clear". Har-har-har)and we quickly tear-
off several goodies, then, I go back to work; in Goodyear truck, don't you know
We'd done this numerous times when the "most homorous" evening came up. It
was a sunday night, so no work, I waited outside 18th and High st. apt. till
parents left and then went in and we fell to it. I had all my clothes off
and in livingroom as she was washing my cock in bathroom,(left this be a
lesson to you, never become seperated from your clothes, at least keep your
trousers handy, when doing this sort of thing in a strange house--oops, my
goodness, Jack, I forgot for a second that you were out of circulation and
certainly not in any need of "Lord Chesterfield's " counciling--don't show
this to your wife, or tell her I offer this extra advice to pass xon to
your son, or, if that's to harsh, to your dilitante friends, whew!, got
out of that) there's a rattling of the apt.'s door(don't think I can't
spell apt.--apartment; yeh-yeh,) and into the front room walks the mother of
one of the parents of the baby C.Mary is watching, so fast did this old bat
come in that we barely had time to shut the bathroom door before she saw us.
Here I was, nude, no clothes, and all exits blocked. I couldn't stay there
for what if the old gal wanted to pee, and most old women's bladders and
kidneys are not the best in the world. There was no place in the bathroom
to hide, nor could I sneak out due to the layout of the apt. Worse, Mary
suddenly remembered the fact that this intruder was expected to stay the nigh
We consulted in whispers, laughing and giggling despite all, and it was
decided Mary would leave the bathroom and keep the old lady busy while
suggesting a walk or coffee down the street and still try to collect my
clothes and get them to me; no mean feat. My task was to, as quietly as a
mouse, remove all the years-long collection of rich peoples bath nicknacks
that blocked the rooms only window, then, impossible tho it looked, I must
climb up the tub to it and with a fingernail file pry loose the outside
screen. Now, look at this window, Jack, it had four panes of glass 8"
long and 4" wide, it formed a rectangle of about 12 or 13" high and 8 or9"
across, difficult to squeeze thru at best, but, being modern as hell, the
way it was hooked to its frame was by a single metal bar in direct center!,
which when opened split the panes of glass down the middle and made two
windows (see below)I could hardly reach outside to work on the screen--since
the window opened outward--but I pushed and making a hellova noise, split the
screen enough to open the window. Now the impossible compressing
of my frame for the squeeze. I thought if I could get my head thru
I could make it; I just was able to, by bending the tough metal
bar the slightest cunthair(in those days I cleaned and jerked 220
lbs.) and, of course, I almost tore off my pride-and-joy as I
wiggled out into the cold November air. I was damn glad I was only
on the second floor, if I'd been higher I would have been hungup
in space for sure. So I dropped into the bushes bordering the walk along
the side of the building, and hid there divering and gloating with glee.
There was a film of snow on the ground, but this didn't bother anything
except my feet until some man parked his car in the alley garage and came
walking past my hideaway, then, much of my naked body got wet as I pressed
against the icy ground so he wouldn't see me. This made me seek better

(14)

sheltersince it was about 9PM--I'd been in the cold an hour--and a whole
string of rich bastards with cars might start puting them away. I waited
until noone was in sight then dashed down the walk to the alley and leaped
up and grabbed the handy drainpipe of a garage and pulled myself up. The
window I'd broken out of overlooked my new refuge and if anyone went in
that bathroom they'd see the havoc wrought the place and looking out see me.
This fear had just formed--I was too cold to be jolly now--when I saw Mary
at last come into view. She had my pants, shoes and coat, but not my T-shirt
and socks, having skipped these small items as she bustled about in front
of the cause of my perdicament"straightening up". The woman had only noticed
my belt and Mary had said she had a leather class at schol and was engraving
it. When I'd bashed out the window Mary had heard the crashing about -The
old lady must have been deaf; while I was escaping kept talking about thank-
giving turkey--and had come in the bathroom to clean up, close the window and
otherwise coverup. I put on my clothes and chattering uncontrolably from
my freezeout walked with Mary to the "Oasis" for some hot coffee. This is
such a sick description of this really funny little scenethat I'm almighty
sorry I put it down; I'm rushing along too fast trying to complete this letter today and am just careless as hell. And so it goes, tale after tale
revolving around this cherry Mary period; here's just a couple more: At
first the mother of this fucking filly confided in me and, to get me on
her side, asked me to take care of Mary, watch her and so forth. After a
while, as Mary got wilder, the old bitch decided to give me a dressing down,
(I can't remember the exact little thing that led up to this, offhand anyhow)
and since she wasn't the type to do it herself--and to impress me,I guess--
she got the pastor of the parish to hand me a lecture. Now, her home was
in one of the elite parishes and so she got the monsagnier --it was a Catholic
church--to come over for dinner the same evening she invited me. I arrived
a little before him and could at once smell something cooking. The slut just
couldn't hold back her little scheme, told Mary to listen closely and began
preaching a little of her own gospel to warm me up for the main event. The
doorbell rang and her eyes sparkled with anticipation as she sallied forth
from the kitchen to answer it. The priest was a middlesized middleaged pink
featured man with extremely thick glasses covering such poor eyes he couldn't
see me until our noses almost touched. Coming toward me across the palatial
livingroom he had his handshake extended and was in the midst of a normal
greeting, the mother escorting him by elbow all the while and gushing introduction. Then it happened, he saw me; what an expression! I've never seen a
chin drop so far so fast, it literally banged his breastbone. "Neal! Neal!,
my boy!, at last I've found my boy!", his voice broke as he said the last
word and his adam's apple refused to articulate further because all it gave
out was a strangled blubber. Choked with emotion,he violently clasped me to
him and flung his eyes to heaven fervently thanking his God. Tremendous
tears rolled down his cheeks, poured over his upthrust jaw, and disappeared
inside his clerical collar. I had trouble deciding whether to leave my arms
hanging limp or throw them around him and try to return the depth of his
feeling with some gesture of my own, I forget just what I did do. But, my
goodness, golly and whooooooeee!, what a sight!! The priest's emotion had
been one of incredulous joyous recognition, Mary's mother's emotion was a
gem of frustrated surprise; startled wonder at such an unimaginable happening left her gaping at us with the most foolish looking face I've ever seen.
She didn't know whether to faint or flee, never had she been so taken aback,
and, I'm sure, didn't think she ever would be, it was really a perfect farce.
Mary and her sister--who was there to lend dignity to her mother's idea--were
as slackjawed as any of us. Depend on sweet Mary to recover first, she did,
with a giggle; which her sister took as a que to frown upon thereby regaining her senses. The mother's composure came with a gasp of artificial goo,
"well! What a pleasant surprise!!", she gurgled with strained smile. This
was as good a coverup as any and I admired her presence of mind, but deplored
that she'd snuck out from under so easily. Oho!, but wait, aha!, she make a
mistake! Her tension was so unbearable--and she had succeeded so well with
her first words--that she decided to speak again, "let's all go into supper,
shall we?" she said in a high-pitched nervous urge. The earnestness of her
tone struck us all as most incongrious and she gave herself away by being
too quick-- since her guest was still holding me tightly.

(15)

The ecstatic priest was Harlan Schmidt ~~was~~ my Godfather when I was baptized
at age 10 in 1936. He had also taught me Latin for some months and saw
me occasionally during the following three years I served at Holy Ghost
church as alter boy. At our last meeting I was engrossed in the lives of
the Saints and determined to become a priest or christian brother, then,
I abruptly disappear down the pleasanter path of evil. Now, 6 1/2 years
later, he met me again in Mary's house as a youth he'd come to lecture.
Well, he didn't get around to the lecture, it never entered his head because it was too full of blissfull joy at finding his lost son. He told
mehow he'd never had another Godson--it just so happened that way--and how
he'd prayed night and day for my soul and to see me again. He could hardly
contain himself at the dinnertable, ~~fidget~~ fidgeted and twittered and
didn't touch his food. He dragged the whole story of the long wait for
this moment out into the open and before the sullen-hearted(she gave me
piercing glances of pure hate when Father Schmidt wasn't looking)mother
actually waxed elequent. When the meal was over the dirtyoldbitch knew
her sweet little scheme had backfired completely for Schmidt at once excused himself, saying he was sure everyone understood, because he wanted
to talk to me alone, and we left. We drove to his church and then sat in
his car for two hours before I got out and walked away, never to see him
to this very day, now five years since. He started in with the old stuff,
and I, knowing there could be no agreement and not wanting to use him
unfairly, came down right away and for once I didn't hesitate as I told him
not to bother; I was sorry for it, but we were worlds apart and it would
do no good for him to try and come closer. Oh we did a lot of talking,
it wasn't quite that short and simple, but as I say, I finally left him
when he realized there was nothing more to be said, and that was that.

The other incident I wanted to tell you about can wait, I must cut
this to the bone from here on out because I haven't the money for stamps.
Anyhow, the reason for this little glimpse into the months just prior to
meeting Joan was to show that there was some cause for what happened to
me in the bar with my younger B.B. Mind you, I hadn't seen Mary's mother
for at least a month before this night in the bar, altho I'd seen Mary
about two weeks earlier. Ah bullshit, whats another few lines, I gotta
break in here and tell you that other funny little thing about C.Mary.
It is this; she was such a hyprocondriac that she often played at Blindness.
Now wait a minute, this was unusual " ybecause she never complained
of illness or anything else, in fact, she didn't complain about her eyes
either, just the opposite, she had a true martyr complex toward them.
Often we'd spent 12-16 hours in a hotel room while she was "blind". I'm
wait on her hand and foot (and cock) during these times. They'd begin
casually enough, she'd simply announce that she couldn't see and that
would go on until she'd just as quietly say she could see again. This
happened while she was driving--I'd grab the wheel--while we were walking--
I'd lead her--while we were loving--I'd finish--in fact, this happened
any old place she felt like it happening. It was a great little game,
she didn't have to worry, if she smackedup the car, or anything, the old
lady would come to the resuue with lots of dough. Oh yes, I forgot, toward
the end she began pulling fainting spells and would pass out equally at
ease on the street or in a bed; my job at these times was to feel her pulse.
Etc, etc, I could go on and on about Cherry Mary, but, enough, and back to
the exciting story of the loss and downfall of my one (ahem) pure love.
If the gentle (or otherwise) reader will kindly bear with me and think
back he might remember that we left our hero snug in his smug little mind
and about to leave a cozy spot on E. Colfax just before 11PM on Xmas eve.

Here they came, I knew it before they'd closed the door behind them,
two big bulls, and heading right for me. "Cassady?", they didn't even look
at younger Bloodbrother, must have had a good description, "come along with
us". Presto! I was back in jail again. (well, so what?, how did I know,
back there on the "gaol" page,that I wouldn't use jail on the next one, I'm
using it now in the place I anticipated for it; damn those long parentheses,
they're calculated to get a poor man off his stroke.) You've surely guessed
it by now(if any of this mess is clear) despite my trying to obtusely keep it
from you. ~~my younger BB had called C.Mary and her mother had arbitrarily vowed.~~

(16)

I was booked for molesting a minor. Before being led to the tank, I knew the way by heart from previous trips, I was brought to the second floor office of a certain police sargeant. You might recall, Jack, a Mr. Paul J. White who is a Los Angles propation officer. I had four seperate rounds with him, I won the first and third and he came out on top in the second and last one. Well, I had the same type of personal duel with this Denver policeman, not exactly the same; White was an absolute shit, the sargeant just a little fart. Trying to think of the name of this guy, to write it down, all I kept coming up with was Giroux(your editor)but I've finally got it; this dicks name is Garrard. Now, I had only two bouts with this jerk, on the first occasion he'd come off best by a big margin; did great work, dug up evidence all over the city to put me away with, here, on the second skirmish, I beat him, but because he wasn't too unfair and let me do it. Sgt. of detectives Garrard worked the night shift, and was second in command to Capt. Childers, who exercised his seniority and worked days. It was near the bewitching hour as I was hauled before old Tom Garrard, a cigar-smoking hard man of 50. He whipped out at me, "where's the money?", I asked him to please come again. "Listen here, you little bastard, I wont take any of your shit, where's the money? I got witnesses that you were in front of the poolhall last nightin a car, and when my witness stuck his head inside the car window he saw the moneybag on the floor. Come on now, where's the money"? I swore I didn't know what he was talking about, and dammit, as luck would have it, I'd done exactly the same sort of swearing when I faced him before, only then I did know what he was talking about and he proved it. Remembering that last time his voice became grimmer and assumed a more threatening tone. "Now listen, you little son-of-a-bitch, I wont take anymore of your lies, so you're just an innocent little punk, huh, well, I'm going to have some of the boys work you over and maybe you wont be so dumb when you get back. I'm tired of your lying". At this he got up,and walking to the door, motioned a big brusier to come take me away. By god, this mystery was getting serious and I was scared enough to shit my pants. "Wait a minute", I pleaded, "Iəll do whatever you say, but I don't know about any money, please explain, honest, I don't know what you're talking about". We were standing in the doorway, he hesitated a moment, then, "OK", and he went back behind his desk and I sat before it with the other dick at my elbow. He told me the poolhall was robbed last night,(the reason I didn't know about it, altho I'd been there the next day, was because the owners had shushed it up so everything would stay normal and give the police a better chance to find out who did it) and I'd been seen in front of the place, after it closed, in a car with this money bag under the seat. This was all true except the moneybag part, but so were a lot of other guys and a few cars and this prick who fingered me for the burglery(money snatched by forcing back door) was full of shit, and just let me face him and prove it. Garrard said he'd see about that and questioned me along these lines, "do you know a Mary Lou Berle? We got her in a home for expectant mothers, and she put in a complaint a few days ago that you raped her". Jesus Christ! How many shocks, happy and otherwise, can a man get in one day? In less than 8 hours I'd been led to Joan, snatched from her, charged with three seperate crimes, the first of which wasn't justified, the second one I knew nothing about, and the third a preposterous lie. Think of it! I hadn't even known M.Lou was pregnant, it certainly didn't show thru her fat, and she claimed I did it. Harrumpph! I sure put that straight in a hurry; told him I hadn't known her a month ago, she'd just come to town, etc, I think he believed me. The pickup had been put out for me on account of this pool hall business and Mary's mother calling the police had been a happy coincidence that Garrard loosened up enough to let out a chortle over. Finally, with a growl to bust my teeth in if he checked the PH story and found I'd lied, he sent me upstairs to the lockup.

When a prisoner is released from COLO. S. Reformatory he is placed on a years probation, and if, among other reasons, he is found in a bar his parole is revoked and he's sent back to do time and a half. Even if I beat all three of these raps, I'd still have that stickler to hurdle. Lying on the inner-steel matteress, I figured my moves in mental shudderings. I had M.Lou whipped at the start, I thought I'd bust the poolhall thing too, C.Mary

might drop charges if I got the priest, Father Schmidt, on the ball. Yep, my
main worry was parole violation and the only hope to escape that laid on
the charity of Sgt. Garrard.

There is a quality of calm, a collected coolness, a careful restraint
that is the foremost feature of the mind when in jail. One is not inclined
to rowdiness, the eyes rove over the cell's fixtures and unconciously
count each bar. Small things assume undue importance and nostalgic longing
permeates every thought. I awoke from a night of bad dreams and was pleased
to feel my usual jail-peace take hold and disperse these phantoms. A treat
was in store, being Christmas day, the prisoners were allowed the freedom
of the corridor. As on ordinary days,from 8 to 4 we had the bullpen to
lounge in too. The gospel-army singers offered 45 minutes diversion by trying to lead the uncooperative jailbirds in a few Protestant hymns. They also
offered to save our souls, using the common preacher's-voice squeal to give
out with their frantic appeals of foolish logic. This type of salvation
uses many artifices on it's audience, one of the most frequently presented,
and most humorous, comes when the insanely earnest young orator steps forward in his thinsoled black shoes and shiny conservative black suit and while
peering thru modern attractive glasses tries to fix his victims with the
intense piercing "John Brown" , offset with humble pitiful pleading, look;
he always carries a black leather new testament in his right hand. He
would begin his little speech so quietly the uninitiated might take him for
a normal person. He sweated to his climax ; the voice rising in progressive
chords. He'd work up to a plateau of minor frenzy, then, drop suddenly to
a low drone of imbecilic meekness. Each pitch reached for a higher wail
of platitudes to the Lord until it's embarrassing volume was so tremendous
that the noise of a quick-escape artist sawing thru the bars would have
been easily drowned. The wall-eyed emphasis he enjoyed best was making it
clear to one and all that he'd sinned worse than any of them. He thought
it particularly important that everyone know he was no dumb goodie-goodie.
Yessir, he knew what he was yelling about, before he'd discovered merciful
Jesus he had sunk to unspeakable depths. But, praise the lord and hallluiha
the holy spirit had spoken to him and showed the evil of his ways. Just
knowing the error of his life wasn't enough, oh lordy-no, he'd had to accept
Jesus into his heart and the erring habits made this a long hard fight.
He despaired of every making heaven until one blessed day he realized he'd
been cheating. Horrors and more horrors! (he shuddered violently and squeeked
in fear) He'd been cheating the lord, and why?, because he'd kept his pride.
It had been a mock surrender to Jesus, he had falsely hidden his pride away
like a miser, nosiree, he didn't want to give that up. But, the lord knew
it and wouldn't leave him alone until tortured conscience bothered him so
there was no longer any way to hold out. Oh, he tried, he sinned right up
to the last moment, but it was no use; the lord conquered, as always. What
peace when he finally abandoned his soul completely to Jesus!! What joy!
hat rapture! And he wanted to tell us that nothing could harm him now that
Jesus was by his side; he fairly evaporated the steel bars with his hot
breath of inter faith. He blew, no doubt about that, he blew to exhaustion
and when he gave up he knew he'd failed to stir us, the cage was still there,
unmolested; each had his own. Stepping back into his group's lineup, sadness
at this fact touched only his lips, the rest of his visible self regained
the composure of a bank clerk. The next to preach to us was the lone young
girl from out the three or four old women and several men stretched so primly
along the bars; the very bars thru which a sick mexican had puked his musgutel
They stood, too, beside the cell where, a few hours before, a poor white man
had given up his ghost to acute alcbholism; I heard his moaning all night and
thought him just ordinarily ill from drink, they found him dead at morning
checkup. (The services are closed, the sermon's over. I was going to give
a nice nasty sketch of a sweet twat urging us villans to join her in Christ.
But no, the idea of that old man expiring in the adjoining cell, with his
cries unanswered, has unnerved me so I can't get sexy. The tale continues--)

The City and County of Denver didn't provide me with the feast heavis
friendly sergis would have I'd anticipated from Joan's generous couple.
The poor food was partialy made up for by a semi-precious treasure I found;
a song-and-dance man in jail. His name I've forgotten, but not his looks.

(15)

He was a near-perfect replica of Danny Kaye, and patterned his patter
after him; this 5 years ago too, when Kaye was just getting in bigtime.
He was really very funny and never at loss for a quip; I'll modify this
because being the only entertainment in sight his antics where hungerily
picked up by me without critimcism, besides, I favored his clowning since
I'd known a similar fool named John Chevrolotti in L.A.,1942. Quick with
the wit from having worked the nightclubs all over the U.S.A., this D.Kaye
also had many crazy charades of prominent people to toss at me. WE became
jailpals and he told me some shady slut btuckup a place and he'd been living
with her and the cops had him for questioning. Bemoaning the fact he'd
lost a good job and fallen to the level of a jailbird he put on such a hilarious show I split with laughter. Summarizing him quickly, I say he so
enliven the place with his comic tragedy that I scarcely had time for any
morbid brooding or serious planning.

But the time for serious thoughts had come, Garrard called me to his
office the day before New Year's, 1946. I tried to ready a spesl to rival
the only speech I'm proud of—my talk-escape from San Quentin in 1944—yet,
knew I didn't have it as I came before his ugly face. Oh jy, oh happy day,
oh unbelievably pretty words. He said I was free!, not now tho, to teach
me a little "respect", as he put it, I was to stay in jail until Jan. 2nd
and miss any NY celebration. That was alright with me, I poured out thanks
because I knew he was being good enough to forget about the parole violation.
After all, he could have sent me up for a minimum of 18 months, he said
earlier he would if he took a mind too whether The poolhall story checked or
not. Evidently it did check for he didn't mention it, His flatfeet told
him what an obvious whore Mary Lou was, so he gave me the benefit of the
doubt there and C. Mary's mother had dropped her charge Xmas day, just teaching me a lesson she told him. (I remember now a big lecture—and this is
highly unusual for Garrard—he gave me on ruining a fine girl from a good
family like Cherry Mary was) So I was free, yippee! I went back upstairs
bubbling.

One other thing I did in that jail, and that was very easy to do considering my exultant condition. I vowed never to be in jail again, I'd
done this before of course, but I mention it here only because I never have.
And perhaps I might be allowed to say that this final vow I somehow knew
would be kept, altho I suspect—as would anyone else—I think now that I
felt that way then only in the light of subsequent events, i.e.. I've been
prison-free ever since. (hastily I add that nowadays I don't feel the
security of this vow being unheld and tho I certainly wont commit any overt
act to land behind bars, Allen's Chance might popup.)

I left jail for the last time on January 2nd at 9 A.M. I went to the
poolhall and bummed breakfast and a shave. I hurried from the barbxershop
to 1627 Lincoln St. My sweet dove had fled, the lady said Joan had waited
3 days for me to return and then went to FT. Collins. Woe for me, I went
back to the poolhall. (listen Jack, I've just gotten a chance for one more
trip on RR, altho I've been cut off for a week, so since I've got to leave
SF within the hour will rush this off to you) I went to Ed Uhl's ranch,
you recall my letters of nonsense to Haldon, I wrote others to Brierly too.
I came back to Denver to pick up a cow for old man Uhl, I was to stay over
night and get the bull(I think it was a bull) back next day. I ran into J.
Holmes, he knew where Joan was, I flipped, I found her. I can't possibly
describe that night, I know I can, intended to, fillup 10 pages with the
"   ion of it. Suffice to say here that she had been back in Denver since
April(early) and it was the Ides of May (I'm not confused) where we had our
48 hours together. She was a whore, I mean she was living as a whore from
one man to another. Paradoxically, her virginal nature was more pronounced
than ever—she asked to kiss my privates—even tho she had learned to make
love mechanically like a whore. I haven't seen her since. But enuf, The End.

I got the letter from Rambler(thats you) and Moe(Johnny boy) and I didn't
say, or didn't intend, "Now that I got Jack married off—" etc, I meant now
that Jack is married, I wouldn't be surprised, or next in line,-Allen and Ansm
eres the horror: you mean you didn't get a letter from me about Dec. 7th?
I wrote a big typewritten one to; Now Honorable Married Man and thought you'd
get it, so put no name on it-damn it- these lttrs mailmen on Xmas rush cant read.

185

Curtis st. from 18th to 28th was my route. It was winter, cold, and in my mind was the excitment of having my new notebook and pencils. I recall my father had a bottle so I expected him drunk, he was. The surprize was Barbara being there also drunk. I laid my books down and sat tracing my name on the cover as they lay in bed and talked cheery to me. They urged me to bed. I was on the inside agaist the wall, B. in the middle, father on the outer edge. He was nosiely sucking her, she kept up a stream of talk. My penis was hard and got harder. I fell into a passion with her back to me. I stabbed at her for some time, she directed my penis into her cunt saying how strange it was to have dad and me love her both at once. I fucked a long time as father passed out and laid inert. I came in her very good and laid against her allnite This is the first time I remember coming. Sept. 1938
I came home from work tired. John was passed out in a livingroom chair, Lucille on the couch. I here cooking sounds from the kitchen and went in. Pauline was frying bacon. I asked her name what she was doing here and she half-drunk shaid she was the new maid. I told her the bacon was burning she said she liked her meat hot. I became hot and pushed her aganist the cuboards, she said I didn't want to fuck herm, she was a whore, I said that was all the better and urged her upstairs, she refused without money I racked my brain then told her I had an invalueable football—8 buck spalding with which I wouldn't part and would redeem it payday. she reluctantly agreed. I went in the bedroom with her and gave her the beatup football, she lifted her dress and laid crossways on the bed . U refused and demanded her clothes off, again reluct she stripped, I got in bed with her. We fucked all nite I came at least 10 times at 3 a.m. lightness came and marvaling at my passion she asked where I'd learned to fuck so good, her cunt was so sore she couldn't stand any more and pleaded rest. she went into her room and slept exhausted.
I waited for the bus that sun. p.M. having two hours relief and was going home to eat. The girl who had made me so hot in class all year walked by, surprized and trembling I stopped her and forced the talk she accepd invite to coke. I talked incessently, showed her parlor tricks and got her to come inside to show we sat in the balcony. As my time approached for work I put my arm around her and we kissed, she responed and I made her promise to sit there util 10 whenel'd be back. Two hours of fears and anticipation at the door taking tickets. I told all the boys. the usher's room was arranged. I got her reluct ant inside we lais on the couch, everyone was watching, I eased her dress up and got it in. I was called for duty and was rushed to come in her. I went to work and she,distraught by others, left.

* Publisher's note: The auction manuscript included this typewritten page. Whether it was intended as part of the original letter remains uncertain.

Illustration of her husband Neal Cassady by Carolyn Cassady

Acknowledgements

We are grateful to Cathy, Jami and John Cassady and the rest of the Cassady family for use of Carolyn Cassady's photography and line-drawings.

The transcription of the letter is by courtesy of Susan Forrest.

We thank the Neal Cassady Estate for permission to publish this important letter in full.